BREAK POINT

by

Garry Michael

Copyright © by Garry Michael

All rights reserved.

This is a work of fiction. Any similarity to actual persons, living or dead, or actual events is purely coincidental.

No part of this book may be reproduced in any form or by any electronic or mechanical means, including information storage and retrieval systems, without written permission from the author, except for the use of brief quotations in a book review.

Cover design: GLR
Editing: Jennifer Griffin
Proofreading: Carlie Slattery
Beta reading: Michael Robert
Formatting: Sophie Hanks

*This book is dedicated to MRZ, the love of my life.
Thank you for everything.*

Contents

Prologue: Travis 6
Chapter One: Ashton 14
Chapter Two: Travis..30
Chapter Three: Ashton 43
Chapter Four: Travis...54
Chapter Five: Travis..64
Chapter Six: Ashton 72
Chapter Seven: Travis.. 81
Chapter Eight: Ashton 86
Chapter Nine: Ashton 88
Chapter Ten: Travis 97
Chapter Eleven: Ashton... 106
Chapter Twelve: Travis.. 113
Chapter Thirteen: Ashton 121

Chapter Fourteen: Travis 127
Chapter Fifteen: Ashton 136
Chapter Sixteen: Travis 140
Chapter Seventeen: Ashton... 152
Chapter Eighteen: Travis 159
Chapter Nineteen: Ashton 165
Chapter Twenty: Travis 169
Chapter Twenty-One: Ashton......................................176
Chapter Twenty-Two: Ashton 185
Chapter Twenty-Three: Travis 193
Chapter Twenty-Four: Ashton..................................... 199
Chapter Twenty-Five: Travis 206
Chapter Twenty-Six: Ashton....................................... 219
Chapter Twenty-Seven: Travis 227
Epilogue: Travis...236

Prologue
Travis

US Open 2019. Men's Final. Fifth set, 5-4, 40-love, championship point.

This is it. The realization of my dream depends on this point. The dream of becoming the first American man since 2003 to win the US Open rests on this final serve.

You've got this, I murmur to myself as nerves take control of my body and mind, which is new for me, by the way. I do not get nervous. Ever. Ice runs through my veins and pressure only fuels my desire.

What the fuck is wrong with me? My hands start to shake involuntarily, and my heart is pounding so hard I'm afraid it will leave bruises in my chest.

The stadium is full, spectators are going wild and I absolutely love it.

Prologue

The fact that these people are cheering for me, rooting for me, wanting me to be their next champion, is intoxicating.

The chants of "U-S-A! U-S-A!" get louder by the second and vibrations are rippling through the stands, signaling impending eruption.

This is what I was born to do and as long as I have this, nothing else matters.

I close my eyes as I listen to the chair umpire quiet the roaring crowd and seize the opportunity to take a deep breath and calm the growing tension creeping into my body. As I do, a memory flashes into my head, and before I can stop it, I'm transported back to when I was eighteen years old.

***

Eight years earlier

"Hey Trav! Are you done training?" I lifted my head to see my best friend, Ashton Kennedy, entering the Seattle Tennis Academy, the place where I spent most of my days practicing and training with my coach. I had been a common fixture on this court for years and today was one of the few days I practiced alone. I hadn't planned on hitting any balls today, but with Ash being in California, this was the most I could do to refrain from texting him every minute of every hour. It's silly how much his absence affected my routines, but this had been the longest time we had spent apart.

"You know I hate it when people call me that," I said, pretending to be annoyed as he walked toward me.

"I know. That's why I do it. Plus, you correct everyone who calls you that but me, so I figured you must like it when I do it," he added with a wink.

God, if that didn't make me smile. He was not lying though, and if I was being completely honest, I actually liked it when he called me that nickname. I rolled my eyes at him when he reached me and started helping me pack up my gear and equipment.

"What are you doing here? I thought you weren't coming back until tonight?" I asked. I knew he had been excited to go to California and visit Stanford. He'd been dreaming about going there since we were kids, and I didn't doubt for one second that he would be accepted. After all, he was the smartest person I knew.

"The college tour finished sooner than planned so I asked my dad if we could change our flight back to Seattle to an earlier time," Ash said, not looking at me. Then, he whispered, "And I missed you."

I would have missed those last four words if I hadn't been paying attention. I felt him lift his gaze to

Prologue

me and when I looked at him, my heart fluttered. He always had that effect on me. I thought it would eventually go away, but time only managed to magnify the feeling.

Our friendship started when his family moved into our neighborhood when we were ten years old. The undeniable connection we had with each other was evident from the moment we met. We hadn't had a clue what it was back then, but one thing was for certain, I only wanted to be around him, and he only wanted to be around me, all the time.

We stared at each other for what seemed like an eternity before I finally broke the contact, cleared my throat and spoke.

"I missed you too."

The short walk to my car was awkward. The air between us was filled with so many unsaid things. Sensing that Ash wanted to say something, I slowed down and glanced over at him. Judging by the look on his face, I knew he was just barely keeping his emotions in check. It was amazing how in tune we were with each other. Words were sometimes unnecessary between us.

I stopped walking and turned to face him. His eyes were glued to the ground as if it was the most interesting sight he had ever laid his eyes on. With my index finger I reached out to slowly lift his chin, ensuring he would hear what I was about to say.

"I wish I could be the guy you want me to be." Tears threatened to fall from the corner of Ash's eyes as he studied my face. "You know I love you and I always will. It's just..." I briefly paused and was unsure how to say what I needed to say. I couldn't lie to him, not when he was this vulnerable. And even if I tried, he would be able to see right through me, so I finally said, "I'm not ready." The intense look of disappointment on his face penetrated my well-developed emotional armor. It was so intense that I forced myself to look away.

"You know your family will support you no matter what. They only care about your happiness. You have to know that," he assured me.

"It's not them that I'm worried about."

"Then what is it?" Ash raised his hands in the air, his frustration and exasperation evident. "Is it me? Don't you want to be with me?"

"No!" I yelled, cutting him off. "It's not you!"

"Then what is it, Travis? What is keeping us apart?"

A lump formed in my throat and prevented me from saying anything as soon as he started sobbing. I hated to see him cry and I hated it even more that I was the reason why. I pulled him into a tight hug, hoping the gesture conveyed all the emotions that my words failed to do. I didn't realize that I was holding my breath until he hugged me back and buried his face in the crook of my neck. I held him there for a while until he gathered himself.

Prologue

"I got you something from California."

"What is it?" I asked, welcoming the change of subject.

Ash pulled something out of his pocket with a sheepish grin and I was immediately thankful to see that gorgeous smile return to his face. Those baby-blue eyes behind his black-framed glasses were something I would never tire of looking into. He had the most amazing blue eyes I had ever seen. The hue was so indescribable that it was easy to get lost in them. Those eyes were the real gauge of his thoughts and emotions, and the weary look that was there just moments ago was replaced with ease.

"It's nothing fancy," he said bashfully, as he showed me a small silver pin in the shape of a tennis racket.

"This is so cool. I love it!"

"This can be your lucky charm. I know you don't need it, but it's good to have."

"Thank you."

"You're welcome. Promise me that you'll wear this for every match. That way you'll know that I am always with you, even if I'm not around."

Suddenly, it felt like my heart was too big for my chest, overwhelmed by the love my best friend had for me and a profound sense of guilt. I knew that leading him on like this was unfair, especially when I didn't have any plans of coming out anytime soon, but I was not willing to let him go yet—or ever.

I gave him a soft kiss on his cheek and whispered, "I promise," knowing all too well that it might be the only promise I would be able to keep for him.

***

The noise of the crowd brings me out of my reverie. I hear them yelling my name, seeming to sense the importance of this moment. The octave of the fans' calls rises 100 amps higher and brings me back to reality.

As I open my eyes, I look up to where my team is sitting. Only they aren't sitting this time—they're on their feet looking as nervous as I am. I take another deep breath to maintain my sense of equilibrium.

You've got this, I tell myself one more time before touching the small silver pin on the collar of my shirt.

I position myself to hit one of the most important serves of my life. I bounce the ball eight times, toss it in the air, then hit a 130-mph ace.

"Game, set, match, Travis Montgomery," the chair umpire announces.

I did it! I drop my racket and kneel on the ground, placing my palms to my face. *I really did it!*

My opponent walks around the net and gives me a hug. "Congratulations, Travis! Great match."

"Thank you!"

I jump up and down with my fists in the air, then wave jubilantly to the crowd. They erupt with energy, and confetti and balloons descend from the roof of the arena. My vision blurs and I realize I am crying. My friends and family hug each other with joy, while an unexpected feeling of longing takes residence in my heart.

An image of Ash appears in my head for a split second and I hope that somewhere out there he is able to see me win. *This one is for you,* I say under my breath as I touch the silver pin on my collar once more.

Chapter One
Ashton

"Yeah! He did it!" I exclaim as I watch Travis win his first US Open. "He finally did it!"

The last four hours have been a rollercoaster of emotions. A maelstrom of them. I was happy, sad, angry and mad—and that was just the first hour. At one point, I found myself yelling like a maniac at the television screen for no logical reason.

Watching Travis' face fill with so much joy and relief as he pumps his fists in the air is a revelation. I know how much winning this tournament means to him. Sure, he's won two Wimbledon Championships and a French Open title over the years, but winning the US Open has been his ultimate dream since we were ten years old. Watching it unfold right in front of me brings an unexpected sadness so strong that tears come to my eyes.

Chapter One

There was a time in our lives when I would have shared this monumental event with him. We'd even thought of how we were going to celebrate. I remember him suggesting partying with chocolates and gummy bears, while I tried to convince him that going to a restaurant and ordering all flavors of milkshakes was the way to go. We surely didn't realize the enormity of this event then, back when we were barely teenagers.

I blink away the tears that are starting to form to stop the cluster of unwelcome emotions forming in my chest.

"Good job, Trav. I am so proud of you."

With the match now over, I am emotionally exhausted. Beads of sweat cause hair strands to stick to my forehead, and the heat emanating from my face fogs up my glasses. I'm sure my complexion is all shades of red by now.

And why are my mouth and throat so dry? Every swallow I take feels like ingesting sand. Oh right. "Because you haven't drunk a drop of water since you sat down four hours ago," I scold myself.

Going through the maze of moving boxes, I reach the kitchen of my new place. Living on a houseboat is a first for me. All spaces on its rectangular shape are designed with purpose. Each corner highlights the sweeping view of the Seattle skyline and the famous Space Needle. And with the setting sun, the city is tinted with an orange glow and gives the water a golden shade. A perfect backdrop for my lakefront position.

The living room is separated from the patio that hangs over Lake Union by floor-to-ceiling nano glass doors that open completely to give an outdoor-indoor living experience. The kitchen is minimally designed, with modern appliances that match the gray stone counter top with swirls of white marble that looks like art itself.

Even with all the furniture wrapped in plastic and stacks of boxes everywhere, it's not hard to imagine all the decorating possibilities I have with this place. Living here is going to be a lot of fun. I make a mental note to call my good friend Dawson and thank him for letting me lease this amazing place.

Mr. and Mrs. Blanchard, Dawson's parents, are two of my parents' best friends, and because of the three-year age difference between Dawson and I, I've always looked up to him like an older brother. He is also the only person who knew the real score between Travis and me. When there was a Travis and me.

Dawson's move to Australia for a man he met while the guy was on vacation in Seattle ended my month-long search for a place closer to the hospital while still being affordable, because there was no way I could have afforded to live in a setting like this on a resident's salary.

Chapter One

It would have been much easier to live in one of the properties my parents own all over the city, but that would mean relying on other people when I promised myself to do this journey on my own.

My parents are not other people; they are great, loving parents and have always been incredibly supportive of my choices. But being their only child means I am the sole recipient of their attention and their unyielding need to be involved in every part of my life, to a fault.

They knew I was gay before I did, so coming out was almost uneventful. I always tease them that they robbed me of that experience and jokingly accuse them of raising me as gay for their own benefit.

But I did manage to complete pre-med and medical school without their help, and I am not about to start asking for help now. It will probably take me decades to pay off my student loans. And just like countless times in the past, I will figure it out on my own.

My face, now dripping with sweat, is greeted by the cold air coming from the refrigerator when I open it to grab a drink. I linger there for a while to stop my body from overheating. And when the fridge alarm starts beeping annoyingly, reminding me that I am single-handedly killing Earth by wasting electricity, I know I need to close the door of the offending machine.

I pass by a full-length mirror that serves to make the place appear bigger and I stand in front of it to study my reflection. I have filled out over the years. I'm not a gym rat by any means, but running and cycling have given me an athletic look. And because of the chronic asthma that has plagued me since childhood, that's about the extent of what I can do physically. Even my hair is different. I no longer keep it short and neat, it now hangs just below my ears with a slight wave, and my time living in southern California has given my pale skin a slight color.

What remains the same are my black-framed glasses. They have been my signature look, even when kids used to call me "nerd" or "dork" when Travis was not around.

My attention lands on my tender lower lip. It's red and swollen from the repeated assault it endured from my teeth during the entire match. I'm not quite sure when and how that habit started, but somehow I find it soothing, especially when I am feeling nervous and stressed.

This is exactly the reason why I don't follow sports. Some people say that watching sports is enjoyable and fun. Well, I beg to differ. The hyperventilating and constant feeling of anxiety are anything but enjoyable and the opposite of fun. I can't believe my father puts himself through this emotional chaos following his favorite football team as they play each week. Just the mere thought makes me exhausted.

Chapter One

I sometimes feel like a fraud pursuing a residency in sports medicine when I clearly don't enjoy some aspects of it. I keep reminding myself that even though I don't enjoy watching sports, I love helping athletes, both amateur and professional, get back to competitive form after an injury. Witnessing the looks on their faces when you tell them they can finally resume training never gets old. I may not be an athlete, but I understand the hard work they endure and the sacrifices they make perfecting their chosen discipline. The countless hours they spend practicing as a child while missing out on activities we deem fun is admirable. And it doesn't end there. They still have to put in the same amount of work, if not more, to enhance that skill to be great.

How do I know this? Not because I am one of those people, but because I lived through it with my best friend. Although I don't think it's right to still call him my best friend, for two reasons. First, we were more than just best friends. We were each other's soulmate. Well, at least I thought we were. And second, we haven't seen or spoken to each other for nearly six years.

Watching Travis' victory today makes me believe that all the camping trips he skipped, summer vacations he missed, birthday parties he forgot, and relationships he broke are worth the success and accolades being thrown at him now.

As my adrenaline starts to dwindle, reality replaces the ecstasy from the excitement of Travis' win. A voice in my head reminds me that I can't share this special moment with him. Not anymore. We're not even friends now.

Unsure of what to do next, I grab my phone from the coffee table and contemplate whether I should send him a text to congratulate him for this momentous milestone of his young career. And before I can overthink it, I tap the screen to bring it to life and scroll down to find Travis' text message from six years ago.

It's pathetic that after all these years I still can't find the courage to delete his text messages. They are the only thing I have to remind me of how things were between him and I. It feels like deleting these messages will be the finality to what we had. And even if it has been six years, I am still holding on to the possibility that someday, somehow, we can at least be friends.

Old insecurity rears its ugly head and the voice in my mind becomes louder, telling me that I will never be enough for him. *That's why he left you six years ago. Remember?*

After typing *Congratulations, Travis!* on the text chain, my thumb hovers around the send button, debating whether I should press it. Against my better judgment, I hit send.

Chapter One

I resume unpacking my things as soon as the cacophony of old feelings stops wreaking havoc on my already fragile state of mind. This distraction is exactly what I need to get Travis out of my system, at least for tonight.

One by one, I unwrap the rest of the furniture and try to position them in a way that maximizes the space and creates a spatial border line between the kitchen and living space. Once I am satisfied with where things are, I tackle the boxes next.

Feeling my motivation start to decline, I grab my phone and open the music app, peruse the selection, and decide to play songs from Taylor Swift's catalog. All right, let's *Shake it Off*.

By the time I finish unpacking the last box containing books, it is well past sundown. I tap the screen of my phone and realize that it's a quarter past ten. After turning off the music, I make my way back to the patio for some fresh air. This part of my new home is becoming my favorite.

Being that it's the tail end of summer, the air is crisp without being too cold. The city and its surroundings are illuminated from a different kind of light than this afternoon. Nightlights now dominate the cityscape, twinkling like stars captivating even the most restless soul. I force myself to sit down and enjoy what little time I have before the beginning of another new week.

I never realized how much I missed Seattle. Moving back home after medical school was always the plan, and getting accepted into the most coveted trauma and sports medicine residency in the nation is the icing on top. But coming back home is stirring all kinds of memories and feelings that I have tried so hard to ignore to prevent my heart from bleeding.

I know that burying my head in the sand isn't the healthiest thing to do when faced with adversities. I know that, one by one, I will have to face these demons. But for right now, I can't get myself to think about anything but Travis and this beautiful view in front of me.

Later, as I open my eyes for the millionth time while lying in bed, it's obvious sleep is not happening tonight, not by a long shot. I have been tossing and turning since I attempted to go to sleep nearly two hours ago.

Even after purposely running myself haggard with chores today, my mind keeps going back to Travis. One glance at the clock on my nightstand tells me it's past midnight. The adrenaline from today's match brings to the surface feelings I thought I had overcome, and the realization that watching Travis on television will bring back the twenty-year-old in me makes me uneasy. And just for tonight, I allow myself to look back and reminisce about a time when life

Chapter One

between Travis and I was the sole driving force of my dreams and future.

***

Eight years earlier

"Are you really going to live in the dorm?" Travis asked.

"Yes, Trav. I am. I would like to have a full college experience, you know."

"I get that. But you can do that while living with me in my apartment. Imagine the fun we can have." He waggled his eyebrows.

"We've gone over this, Trav. The only way you can convince me to live with you is if we're going to do it as a couple. I can't be your roommate—and I'm also not going to force you to do anything you're not ready for. This is your own journey, and I will support you along the way." I saw his smile falter and the playful look on his face was replaced with what I can only assume was worry. The look that always followed these kinds of conversations, and just like in the past, I ignored it, fearing what was behind his worry. "Plus, I thought your mom was going to ask your cousin to be your roommate."

"I know. Don't remind me."

"How is Sawyer, by the way? I haven't seen him in a couple of years."

"He's fine, why are you asking?"

"I'm actually hoping to ask him about medical school." Travis gave me a knowing look and raised his eyebrows.

"What? I really want to ask him a few questions about the MCAT and my med school application," I said with a grin. "Besides, I intend to marry a Montgomery, and since you and I are a big *no*, I have to start sending feelers out there, you know. Your brother, Cole, is straight, so he's out of the picture. That leaves Sawyer. What do you think?"

Travis narrowed his eyes and started heading toward the hallway. I was about to say I was sorry and that I was just teasing him, but I quickly realized that he wasn't leaving.

He was locking the door.

The sound of a metal chain clunking against the door echoed around the room. He paused for a moment before he looked back at me from over his shoulder with a sinister grin. The look of desire in his eyes was enough to make me shiver and melt at the same time.

Travis kicked off his shoes one by one. He undid his belt and pulled his shirt over his head, exposing his muscular physique, and then he winked and took a couple of steps forward. He unzipped his jeans and

Chapter One

leaned over to pull his socks off. He stood back up and his jeans slid off his athletic hips. He continued to walk toward me with a slow pace and never broke eye contact, wearing nothing but his underwear. He was so damn sexy. His six-pack abs were a perfect complement to his bulging biceps and solid, muscular chest. He reminded me of a predator about to claim its unsuspecting prey, only I was willing prey, because when it came to Travis, I was whatever he wanted me to be.

I countered every forward step he took with a backward step of my own until there was no place for me to go. I found myself sandwiched between the concrete wall and the wall of sinfully delicious muscle that was Travis. He grabbed my wrists and raised them over my head. Excitement filled me. He pressed his body on mine, teasingly, as he whispered, "So? Sawyer, huh? You want to run that by me again?" His voice was low, airy, and so seductive it sent tremors through my whole body, and for the first time that day I was speechless.

He pulled his boxers off and ground his growing erection against my hip as he kissed me. The kiss started sweet and eventually turned hungry and wet, accompanied by tongue. The fire I saw in his eyes a minute ago was now a full-on inferno.

He broke the kiss for a second to pull my shirt off

while keeping my hands over my head. "Keep them there," he ordered.

The moment the offending garment hit the floor he was back on me with a frenzy. His hands roamed all over me, exploring every inch of my naked torso. A moment later they were replaced by his lips, which aggressively moved down my neck to my collarbone and then my abdomen.

Travis yanked my gym shorts down; my dick was swelling quickly from anticipation. I brought my hands down, one resting on his head and one on his shoulder, hoping to direct his mouth to my erection. The head of my cock pulsated with need as he put his hands under my balls and gently pulled. With every tug, my cock came closer to the bullseye I craved.

Travis was apparently in no hurry as he licked the smooth skin on my hips, narrowly avoiding what I was trying to feed him. I tensed and flexed my thick cock in anticipation of his warm mouth. My cock's head was swollen and purple, angry at the lack of attention. He lifted my sack to his mouth and swept his tongue across my balls, stopping at the base of my cock. "Mmmm, that's it...come on," I begged. I removed my hand from his shoulder and placed both of my hands to the side of his face. *I guess I'll have to guide my cock myself,* I thought.

"Don't rush me or I'll stop," he teased.

Chapter One

"Don't you dare!" I plead. Travis finally slid his tongue up the underside of my shaft and stopped at the head of my cock. He teased the slit and I gasped from finally getting my wish. I held his head tightly as I tried to maneuver my dick into his mouth, but he kept turning away and teasing the head. The more I thrusted my cock toward the prize, the slower he got around to fulfilling my aching desires.

I decided to lean back against the cool cement wall, so I removed my hands from his head. Travis continued his unfair torment on the head of my cock while gently rolling my nuts in his hand. I was acutely aware that my cock would make its own decisions about coming if he didn't open his sexy mouth soon. He was turning me on, and he knew it. I tilted my head back and closed my eyes, letting myself enjoy the slow dance, and that was when his mouth came down around my throbbing dick. Warmth surged through me at finally being drawn into his mouth.

He began taking me as deep as he could. After the painful wait, I felt my load building up and I grabbed his head again. I moved a hand to the back of his head and applied force, and he accepted every inch of me. Travis got the hint and applied more pressure to my cock with his hand, its twisting motion increasing. "That's it, Trav," I moaned, while my hips squirmed with the anticipation of what was coming soon.

Travis opened his eyes and looked up at me. I noticed he was busily palming his own thick cock and the erotic image got me even hornier and sent me over the edge. My eyes rolled back into my head from the pleasure. "Oh yeah, that's it," I growled, slamming my dick into his mouth faster and harder. "Yes...that's right, yes, yes, don't stop, Trav!"

I was working myself into a frenzy and knew I was seconds away from blasting my load into his waiting throat. I gripped the back of his head and forced him to accept his prize. I moaned as my cum exploded, but Travis didn't release my dick. He kept milking it and a low, rumbling growl escaped him as he sprayed jets of his own cum on the floor.

We rested for a few minutes before we made love. It was slow and tender this time around. We explored each other like we had forever. And after the next time we were exhausted, and finally gave in to our aching bodies.

I felt at home there, lying with Travis. A place where there was no fear, pain, or chaos. Just him and I.

"I love you," Travis said, before finally falling asleep.

***

Chapter One

I lie awake in bed for a few more minutes until I feel the slight rocking of the houseboat caused by ripples from the late- night breeze. I didn't know how to feel about that at first. It seems disconcerting to have your home move under your feet. But now, it feels like a lullaby, especially during these nights when sleep eludes me. A few more minutes pass before my eyelids grow heavy. I close my eyes, with Travis the last thought in my mind.

Chapter Two
Travis

Being a professional tennis player allows me to travel to the most spectacular places and exotic locations in the world. Each of them provides different experiences unique to its own people and culture. But no matter how hard I try to put down roots, the notion loses its appeal faster than I entertain it. Sure, I've made good friends and established relationships along the way, but the closest thing I've done that resembles settling down is purchase my apartment in New York City. This is where I reside during the occasional time off that my team forces me to take, and during the two weeks when the US Open is being held in late summer every year.

The space is nothing fancy—a two-bedroom, two-

Chapter Two

bathroom industrial unit—but it still cost me a good amount of my savings. What sold me on the place was the view of the skyline along the water that reminds me of the place where I grew up. The place where Ash and I grew up. I curse my brain for allowing myself to think about him again. For whatever reason, he's been on my mind these past few days.

To say that the day after the US Open is hectic is the understatement of the year. I barely sleep five hours before I force my tired ass out of bed to get ready for the series of television appearances, magazine interviews, and photo shoots that my agent, Aaliyah Gates, lines up for me. I don't mind it. Being a public figure is part of the job. There are times when I wish I could have some privacy, especially after a tough loss when all I want to do is get wasted or walk around the city without being hassled by paparazzi or fans. But it's the price we pay, and we all learn to deal with it.

Aaliyah has been representing me since I joined the tennis pro tour right after college. I remember feeling overwhelmed by the sheer amount of work off the court the agency required me to do. But with her help, I learned to navigate the complexity of the business.

Unlike most of the relationships I have with my team, we're also great friends. She's rescued me from a number of sticky situations over and over again. And for that, she deserves an actual medal or perhaps a statue erected for taking me as a client, because let's face it, working with me is not a cakewalk. And as though my mind conjures her presence, the sound of a key unlocking my door gets my attention.

"I hope you're decent!" Aaliyah announces as she enters my loft.

"No, I'm not!" I yell back, knowing it will not deter her from coming in anyway. Proving my point, I see her round the corner of the hallway, cheerful as usual, wearing a mustard-yellow dress that complements her brown skin. I shake my head. "You're gross. No one should be this perky at 6 a.m."

I pour a cup of coffee and hand it to her. Without hesitation, she gives me a kiss on the cheek and takes a quick sip, following it with a contented sigh. I look at her. "You know those keys are for emergency, right?" I emphasize the word *emergency*.

With an exaggerated shrug, she waves her hands at me as if I said something inconsequential. "This is an emergency." She takes another sip of coffee before continuing. "I am not about to let you be late to your first appearance on *Live with Kelly and Ryan.*" The comical look on her face is almost enough to brighten my day. Almost. "Do you even know what you're going to wear?" She pauses for another sip. "And who is going to do your hair?"

"My hair? What's wrong with my hair?" I ask,

Chapter Two

crossing my arms to feign irritation. "I will have you know that my hair once started a trend. It even went viral."

"Yes, your hair. This," she continues as she motions her hand all over the hair in question, "is not happening today. And what trend? Do you mean when two other tennis players copied your look because they both lost a bet?" She makes air quotes at the word *copied*. She's on a roll now. Enjoying this banter, I let her continue. "No, I don't think so. It's bad enough that I let you do your press conferences with this disheveled look. And you have me mistaken for someone else if you think for one second..."

"Okay, okay, I get it, it's an emergency," I surrender, raising my hands in the air. "Sorry for questioning your intentions." And before I can help it, a big laugh escapes my mouth.

"Thank you. Now finish your coffee. We have work to do," she commands.

"Don't you have other clients to boss around this early?"

"I do. But none of them just won the US Open." Her eyes warm with sincerity as she walks toward me and gives me a hug. "I'm really proud of you."

"Thank you. I couldn't have done this without you."

"I've always believed that you could do it. Even during those days when you didn't."

I smile. Preventing this encounter from going from snarky to weepy this early, I excuse myself to take a quick shower before we leave.

A black BMW 7 Series sedan is waiting for us as we exit the lobby of my apartment. An older man in a suit comes around from the driver's seat to greet us and opens the back-seat door for Aaliyah, as I go around to get in the other side.

"This is fancy," I whisper as we get in. The interior of the car screams luxury. The soft leather seats are separated by a middle console that has buttons to control pretty much everything inside. The obviously expensive wood trim gives the car a sophisticated finish, and the video screens built in to the backs of the passenger and driver seats are high tech and very on-brand with the car.

"I forgot to give you something upstairs, but promise me you won't make a big deal about this, okay?" I ask.

Aaliyah gives me a curious look as she buckles up. "It depends on what it is," she replies.

"Oh, forget it."

"I'm just kidding. You are *so* not a morning person."

I hand her a medium-sized box wrapped in matte-black paper with a shiny silver bow.

"I've been meaning to give you this, but I got too busy with my training for the Open. This is my thank you for always being there for me and being such a good friend.

I wouldn't be where I am without you," I explain.

"The wrapping is so pretty!" She begins to unwrap the present, first pulling the bow off and then dramatically tearing the paper. A green box is revealed; her eyes widen and her jaw drops when she reads the label.

"Rolex! Oh my god, Travis, Rolex?" She slips the box open to find a platinum watch with a pink face. She starts tearing up, which is something I've never seen her do before.

She unbuckles her seatbelt, lunges toward me, and gives me a kiss, followed by her signature tight hug.

"Travis, thank you."

"You're welcome. Now let's get this party started," I say, and she gets the hint that I don't want this moment to be too deep.

The City that Never Sleeps is a perfect moniker for New York City. The streets are already buzzing with activity, even this early in the morning. Yellow cabs flood the streets, and men and women in business attire swamp the crowded sidewalks in a mission to get somewhere fast.

While the traditional shops are still closed, most of the street vendors have already claimed their spots, selling coffee and all kinds of morning delights, from pastries to breakfast sandwiches.

At eight o'clock in the morning, we arrive at the ABC

studio at Lincoln Square on the Upper East Side. The drive from my apartment to the studio takes twenty minutes, and with ninety minutes before my appearance, I ask, "Aren't we a little early?"

"Early? We're almost late," she says.

"But I thought my appearance was scheduled for 9:30 a.m?"

"It is, but remember about the whole makeover thing?"

"Makeover? You said a haircut!"

"Travis, can we not fight about this? Trust me, this is important."

"Important how? Will it solve famine?"

"No."

"Cure cancer?"

"Travis!"

"No, seriously, how important is it?"

"Can you just please trust me on this one? When have I given you ill-guided advice?"

I don't have to think about that last statement, since I know the answer is an unequivocal *never*. Aaliyah might be a pain in the ass sometimes, but she only wants what is best for me. There aren't a lot of people who I can say that about. I've been burned many times by fake friends who use me to get invited to parties or meet other celebrities. It's hard not to take it personally, but those experiences only

Chapter Two

make me appreciate the relationship I have with her more.

I finally cave as we enter the revolving glass door to the spacious lobby. "Okay, but if they make me look like a clown, you only have yourself to blame." The smile on her face when she realizes I'm all in is the only sign I need to know I made the right decision.

After passing by the security team, who hand us our badges for the day, we head upstairs where the *Live with Kelly and Ryan* studio is located. We pass through a narrow hallway with several doors. Two are offices for Kelly and Ryan, as indicated by their nameplates. Aaliyah tells me that those offices are actually dressing rooms, and the one further down the hall with *Guest* written on a gold star is where we are headed.

A very flamboyant guy greets us as we enter the room. He is dressed in a loose gold silk shirt featuring a medusa printed in the center, and is wearing the tightest black jeans I have ever seen. He extends his arm for a handshake as he introduces himself. Although, I'm not sure if I can call that a handshake since it's more of a...I really don't know what it is. Maybe he expects me to kiss his ring?

My head jolts up and I immediately put on my best poker face to prevent myself from laughing out loud and ultimately offending him when he announces his name is Butch. I wait to see if he's kidding, but after he directs his attention from me to Aaliyah, I look around to see if there are hidden cameras or if I'm being Punk'd. After waiting for a few moments and no one tells us we are, I conclude he must be for real. When Butch excuses himself to get something next door, we lose our ever-loving shit.

After I sit for almost an hour in front of a mirror framed with light bulbs, Butch indicates he's finished and looks at Aaliyah. She gives him her final approval.

"Sweetheart, you will give those models a run for their money," Butch says.

"Amen, Butch, amen!" Aaliyah jokes.

The interview goes as planned. Kelly and Ryan introduce me as the new world number-one tennis player and 2019 US Open champion. I enter the stage carrying the iconic US Open trophy while upbeat music plays, and then I exchange pleasantries with the hosts.

"So how does it feel being the number- one tennis player in the world?" Ryan asks as soon as we are seated.

"It hasn't sunk in yet."

Kelly, sitting beside me, lays her hand on my knee. "Travis, congratulations on winning the US Open. I have a question for you. I noticed you paused for a moment before serving that last point. What was on your mind when you were serving for the match? Did you think about the last two US Open finals?"

"You mean the last two finals I lost?" I tease.

"Oops, sorry, but yes."

"No, I didn't think about them. I was thinking of something outside of tennis throughout the entire match, a time when I was happiest. Especially when I was down and needed motivation to keep fighting through. That seems to be what made the difference this year. And clearly it worked," I say, lifting the trophy to prove my point. The audience laughs and starts cheering.

"So, Travis, was it a special someone you were thinking of the whole time? Who is she?" Kelly pushes after the applause dies down.

"Yeah, who is the special lady?" Ryan adds.

My whole body tenses with that question. This probably makes me the scummiest person on the planet, but this is the part when I lie. Automatically, I prepare one of my many well-rehearsed answers. What does that say about my character?

With a straight face, I look at Kelly and Ryan and say, "I haven't found her yet, but I know she's out there."

The collective *oohing* and *awwing* reverberates through the studio, and judging by the hosts' reactions, I know they're satisfied. A couple more safe and routine

BREAK POINT

questions are thrown my way until the producer, Gelman, finally gives us the warning for a commercial break.

"Thank you so much for dropping by today," Ryan says once we're off air.

"Please come back again soon. It was a real pleasure," Kelly says as she gives me a hug.

After saying our goodbyes, I walk out of the studio as fast as I can. I pass by Butch and he says, "Nice interview, Boo."

Wanting to avoid being an ass to someone who's been exceedingly kind to me, I touch his shoulder and murmur a sincere, "Thank you."

I keep walking and as soon as Butch is out of sight, I run. Aaliyah calls out my name, but I don't stop. I know I need to get out of here and fast.

I take a deep breath as soon as I'm outside.

"Are you okay?" I hear her behind me.

"Yes. I wasn't feeling good all of a sudden. I'm still fatigued from yesterday."

"Are you sure? Should we call Drew?"

"No. I'll be fine." Drew is my trainer and physio who helps me recover after a grueling match like yesterday. "I just need some fresh air."

"Fresh air in New York City?" I can sense her trying to lighten the mood. "Our car is right around the corner, let's get out of here."

Chapter Two

She leads us to the spot where the car is parked. The drive to my apartment is quiet and I'm thankful that Aaliyah recognizes I'm not in the mood to discuss what just happened. Hoping that she buys my initial excuse, I push my luck.

"Do you think we can reschedule the rest of the day? I think I need another day to rest."

"Of course. Do you think you'll be fine tomorrow?"

"Yes, I do."

"Then that's what we'll do."

Expecting resistance, I look at her to see if she is truly okay rescheduling the whole day just hours before our other engagements. The look of sincerity and concern I see on her face assures me that she is.

"I'm sorry," I say. "I hope no one gives you a hard time."

"If they do, I'll call Butch," Aaliyah replies.

An uncontrollable laughter possesses me, and it lasts long enough to make my stomach hurt. I continue laughing and for some reason I can't stop until my laughter is replaced with silent sobs.

Aaliyah wraps her arm around my back and her other hand curls around my neck, cradling my head. Before I can protest, she pulls me into her chest. She whispers, "You're okay. Everything is going to be just fine, honey."

I don't know how long we're in that position but

when I look up, the car has stopped in front of my place. I take a few deep breaths to compose myself.

"I'm sorry," I say, without looking her in the eye.

"Don't be. Are you going to be okay? Do you want me to cancel everything for the week and schedule your flight to Seattle earlier?"

There is nothing I would rather do than go back to my parents' house and get some rest and a break from all of this, but I know that's unfair. Not just for Aaliyah, but for everyone who has helped me get to where I am. Also, my fans are hoping to get a glimpse of their US Open champ. But I know that she will cancel everything if I ask her to.

"No, I'll be okay. I promise. I just need a little break is all."

"Okay, but if you feel like this is too much, just call me, okay?"

"I will. Thank you. For everything."

"Of course. I'm always here for you. You know that, right?"

I nod my head because I know it's true. I step out of the car and go inside the building to a place where I don't have to lie, where I can be my true self.

Chapter Three
Ashton

Those doctors who recommend eight hours of sleep every day clearly aren't surgeons. Nothing against them really, but I would take any amount of sleep at this point.

As first-year residents, the shifts we're given are either evenings, weekends, or holidays. It's almost like a rite of passage, an initiation that separates the weak from the hardcore. Where I fall within that spectrum is still up for debate. There are days when medicine flows out of me like second nature and there are times when I feel like I have no clue what I'm doing or if I've chosen the right vocation.

After changing out of my scrubs to the clothes I wore the night before, my phone alarm starts beeping, catching me off guard and disrupting the silence in the locker room. I try to turn it off as quickly as I can, but instead my phone drops to the floor. "Damn it," I curse as I pick it up and read the notification on the screen. It's a reminder about breakfast with my friend Katie.

I make my way from the hospital to our favorite breakfast café near campus in record time. The place is nothing fancy, but they make a pumpkin loaf and coffee cake that are to die for. And to validate my claim, three police officers come in immediately after me and that makes me smile.

The scent of fresh- brewed coffee engulfs the small dining space and instinctively I inhale the smell. After a quick perusal of the place, I spot Katie and join her in the corner facing the small garden.

"How did you get this spot?" I ask after I kiss her on her cheek.

"Timing is everything, sweetie. By the way, I saw you checking out those cops."

"What?" I'm shocked that she even noticed. "I wasn't checking them out." And I wasn't. Truth be told, I haven't been physically attracted to anyone since Travis. I've had multiple opportunities to go out on dates, but I can never find the courage nor the excitement to follow through.

"I saw you smile at one of them. The blond cop for sure," she says.

Chapter Three

"Oh my god, you should be thankful that I showed up."

"Jeez, Ash, you're grumpier than usual. Anyways, when was the last time you went out on a date?" She studies my face, waiting for an answer.

"What kind of question is that?" I reply while waving my hand to get the waitress' attention our way. If this breakfast is going where I think it's going, I'm going to need coffee. Lots and lots of coffee.

"It's a very simple one, Ashton." She sounds so serious that it catches me off guard, but the humor in her eyes betrays her intention.

"You sound like my mom, Katherine," I say, putting emphasis on her full name.

"Oh, don't you sass me!"

I roll my eyes at her fake annoyance. Katie and I have been friends for almost five years. We met during our first year of medical school at UCLA and we connected instantly. She has the type of personality that draws you in. Her ability to command a room with her charm without being obnoxious is something I can only dream of. She reminds me so much of Travis (with a different anatomy, of course), which is the reason why we get along so well.

I remember meeting her for the first time during our medical students' orientation. During that time, I was still reeling from my breakup with Travis two years earlier, and I wasn't always a good friend. I was mentally and physically absent much of the time, but Katie never gave up on me. And I'm glad she didn't because I don't know what I would have done these past few years without her.

"Ash, where did you go?" Katie interrupts my thoughts.

"Did you say something?" I need a cup of coffee right now before I mention something I'm not ready to discuss.

"I said, I've known you for five years and I have never once seen you go out with someone. Why?"

This conversation is heading toward dangerous territory and I'd better find a way to change it, quick. I don't have a problem letting Katie in, there have been many times when I wish I could have shared my past with her, but I can't do that, not without outing Travis.

"Don't even think about changing the topic either," she adds, eerily reading my thoughts.

"I didn't have time then and I definitely don't have time now," I protest, just as the waitress makes her way to our table. It's not a complete lie, but it's the best I can do without spilling my guts before breakfast. It seems to pacify her, but her look says we aren't finished.

"How was the hospital last night? Any interesting cases?" Katie asks.

Chapter Three

"The unit was busy, and we had two surgical fractures that came in the ER. We literally just finished one about an hour ago."

"Oh my god, you haven't slept?"

"Nope, and I have to do rounds in a couple of hours."

"No, you're not. How about you go home and I'll do your rounds for you," she offers.

"I can't have you do that. I still owe you a day for covering for me while I moved."

"You don't owe me anything. You've covered my butt plenty of times. This might be a foreign concept to you, but that's what good friends do. Research it."

"Hey, I am a good friend. I put up with you."

"Aww, you say the sweetest things," Katie mocks.

Our order arrives and we focus our attention on our meals.

"I sometimes wonder why I chose to be a surgeon," Katie says through a mouthful of pumpkin bread. "Don't get me wrong, I love what I do, but sometimes it's just too much."

It is overwhelming at times—the crazy hours, the constant studying, and the fear of doing something wrong that could potentially harm another human being is incredibly stressful—but my reason for choosing sports medicine is deeply personal. Something that I haven't shared with anyone.

***

Seven years earlier

"Trav!" I yelled as I ran from the bleachers to the back of the court the moment I saw him trip and land on his knee. His teammate, Henry, was already by his side when I got there and, out of instinct, I pushed him aside to check on Travis.

I started to feel short of breath from my quick dash to get to him, but I was able to keep an asthma attack at bay after taking a series of slow and steady breaths—an exercise I'd learned from my doctor to get my attacks under control. It wasn't always successful, but I'm thankful that it worked this time, as I didn't have my inhaler with me because I hadn't refilled my prescription.

"Are you okay?" I asked once I focused my attention on Travis, but he didn't respond. His eyes were closed, and the pain etched on his face was something I had never seen before. I thought he might cry. He raised his lower leg to see if he could bend it, but the attempt made him yelp and I started to panic. "What's wrong?"

I wanted to cradle him and assure him that everything was going to be fine, but I knew better. It was the only rule we'd had since we were younger. No public affection.

Chapter Three

"My knee buckled when I was running to hit that last shot," he said with a grimace.

"How bad is it? Would you like to see if you can stand?" Henry asked this time.

"I don't know." Travis extended his arms, silently asking me to help him stand up. He used his right leg, the good one, to prop himself up and he wrapped an arm around my shoulder as soon as he was standing on one leg. I felt him squeeze my shoulder once he had his balance. I knew the gesture meant *thank you, I'm glad you're here.*

Gingerly, he started to put pressure on his injured leg, and cried out at the pain. We lost our balance for a split second as Travis reflexively tried to grab his injured leg. With both of our momentums pulling us to the ground, Henry caught our fall and helped us back to our feet.

"We need to go to the emergency room right now," I urged, as buckets of sweat from his training dripped down his face. As we headed toward his car, Travis looked at me, concern written all over him. There was nothing I wanted to do more in that moment than to kiss him and ease his pain. "Everything is going to be okay," I managed to say.

I'd driven Travis' car multiple times but never when someone else was in the passenger seat. We decided to have Travis lay across the back seat so he could stretch his leg, which meant having Henry next to me. I wished he had stayed back but he was just as concerned for his teammate as I was, and I knew I would need his help getting Travis out of the car. I glanced at Travis in the rear-view mirror and saw him punching the seat, murmuring something incoherent.

"We're almost there, Trav," I said, trying to get him out of the state he was in, but I didn't think it made a difference.

The drive to UCLA Medical Center didn't take long, since the athletic training center where they were practicing was on the other side of the main campus. We parked the car near the entrance of the ER, and I asked Henry to get us a wheelchair. As soon as he left, I pulled the driver's seat forward and leaned into the back of the car to kiss Travis' forehead and tell him once again that everything was going to be alright.

Henry said his goodbye once we were checked in and, after three hours of waiting, the ER doctor made an appearance.

"What does someone have to do to get help around here? We've been waiting for over three hours," I barked. My question was met with nothing but a glare and that made me even angrier.

After performing what seemed to be the fastest physical examination in the history of medicine, the doctor ordered an X-ray, and I was about to ask another

Chapter Three 51

question when the nurse rolled Travis out of the room to take him to the radiology department.

I sat there fuming about how dismissive the doctor had been toward Travis and I. We deserved better than that. Travis might just be another face to him, but this injury could alter his future and an ounce of sympathy would have been nice.

Travis was rolled back into the room as soon as the X-ray was completed, and we waited for another hour. This waiting game was starting to piss me off.

I made an excuse to Travis about using the bathroom, but when I was out of his sight, I went in search of the nurse who helped us earlier. It didn't take long for me to find the nurses' station and I recognized the one behind the counter and caught her attention.

"Hello, I'm with Travis Montgomery, the one with the leg injury in room fourteen. We were just wondering when will the doctor see us?" I tried to sound less agitated.

"The doctor will be with you shortly. It's been terribly busy this afternoon and we're prioritizing who gets seen first," she said without looking at me.

"Do you at least have any idea how much longer we have to wait?"

"I don't," she said, barely acknowledging me.

"Can he get anything for his pain?" I asked, my level

of agitation rising again because of the helplessness I felt.

"I can't give him anything until the doctor sees him."

"But you just said you don't know when that will be!" I heard my voice getting louder and the longer I stood there, the angrier I got.

"Sir, you need to calm down." At least she managed to look at me this time.

"Calm down? We've been waiting for almost five hours and we've seen the doctor once during that time. My friend is in a lot of pain and you haven't given him anything to help with it. We aren't asking for the moon here." I saw a couple of security guards heading in my direction, so to avoid being kicked out of the ER, I lowered my voice.

"Can you please let the doctor know that he is in a lot of pain?" I pleaded, before heading back to the room.

Another thirty minutes had passed when the doctor came back to give us the result of the X-ray. I noticed the same nurse carrying a container with what I assumed was a painkiller. She handed it to Travis, and I gave him the bottle of water I had purchased from the vending machine on my way back to the room.

"Thank you," Travis said with a gritted smile.

"Your X-ray looked fine, Mr. Montgomery," the doctor said, delivering the news as if reciting something off of a cereal box. "But the physical exam

Chapter Three

suggests that you might have torn your ACL. We'll need to get an MRI to rule that out. Once we are one hundred percent sure it's your ACL, I'm afraid that you'll need to have surgery to repair it."

To my surprise, Travis seemed to take the news well. He listened carefully as the doctor gave him the plan and answered his questions about recovery.

Travis was subdued during the short drive from the emergency room to his apartment. His attention was focused on the streets around him and he didn't say anything until we reached the garage.

"Coach is going to kill me. My season is done."

"You don't know that," I argued.

"What if they can't fix me?"

"Trav, ACL reconstruction is very common."

"But what if I have the surgery and I can't get back to where I am. What if I can't...what if I can't play tennis anymore?"

"Let's not get ahead of ourselves. Why don't we go inside, and you can rest? You can call your parents too."

"Will you call your mom to ask for any recommendations?" he asked.

"Of course," I said, even though the last thing I wanted to do was speak to my mother.

Chapter Four
Travis

The captain's voice from the open cockpit door instructing us to fasten our seatbelts signals that we are about to arrive at our destination. The flight from NYC to Seattle took a little more than five hours, and with the time difference we manage to arrive at Seattle's airport before noon.

As I peek outside from the small airplane window, a familiar sense of joy and excitement wraps around my heart like a soft warm blanket on a cold stormy night. It feels like home. Home that always gives me a sense of comfort and security that I cannot seem to find anywhere else, home where my happiest memories live, home where I had my first kiss, home where I fell in love, and home where my heart was broken six years ago. Shaking my head, I focus my

Chapter Four

attention more on the scenery than on the man responsible for my broken heart.

It appears to be nice and sunny outside, odd considering it's the last week of September. Leaves still cover most of the trees, albeit slightly lighter due to the change in evening temperature. "I can't believe it's fall." Weather in the Pacific Northwest, particularly here in Seattle, is notoriously unpredictable. It rains in July and August when the whole nation is experiencing a heatwave, and it's fifty degrees and sunny when the rest of the continental US is powering through an arctic blast.

But what can I say? I love unpredictability and that is way different from Ash. I chuckle at that. And just like that, I'm back to thinking about him. "Fuck," I groan. I really need to get a grip and stop obsessing about him. I unbuckle my seatbelt and stretch my arms and legs as I fish my cellphone out of my back pocket. No sooner than I turn the airplane mode off do notifications of text messages start flooding my screen. I scroll down. With a huge smile, I start with the message from my mom.

Mom: *Hi son! Hope you had a great flight home. Let me know when you arrive.*

Mom: *Cole will be picking you up so call him.*

Mom: *I can't wait to see you.*

I fire off a quick reply letting her know that I've

arrived, then I unload the overhead storage bin of my suitcases. Once I'm off the plane, I read the text from my older brother, Cole.

Cole: *Hey champ! I arrived here earlier than expected so I'm parked in the cell waiting lot. Call me when you're ready.*

Cole: *It will probably take me about ten minutes to get to the arrival gates from here so text me when you have all your bags.*

I dial Cole's number and he picks up after just one ring.

"Welcome home, buddy!" Cole greets me cheerfully.

"Hey Cole! It's nice to be home," I say, matching his excitement. "I'm walking toward the arrival gate now so I should be there by the time you pull up."

"How about your luggage?" Cole asks.

"I have them."

"Already? There must not have been any lines." Cole sounds confused. I hesitate for a moment, debating whether to tell him that I flew to Seattle via private jet. He is going to give me so much shit. In the end, I decide to tell him the truth. I've told plenty of lies this week and I am not about to give my brother another one.

"I chartered a plane," I blurt while bracing myself for the barrage of sarcasm sure to come my way. To my surprise, the statement is met with such silence that I

Chapter Four

actually think the call has dropped. "Cole, are you still there?" I ask after a couple of seconds.

"Oh, I'm still here," he says. The tone of his voice is laced with mischief. "I just thought you said you chartered a plane." It's exactly the way he used to tease me when we were growing up. I roll my eyes at that.

"Fuck off," I say, laughing. I hear Cole chuckle as he says, "I miss you too. See you in a bit, big shot."

After loading my luggage in the trunk of Cole's SUV, we begin the thirty-minute trek to our family home in Queen Anne, a well-established neighborhood in Seattle.

"I'm proud of you, Travis," Cole says once we enter the freeway. "I know how much winning that tournament means to you. I'm sorry I wasn't able to be there. Caitlyn has been having a tough pregnancy and I didn't want to leave her and the two kids alone."

Cole's subdued demeanor catches me off guard and I notice for the first time since I arrived that he looks tired. Dark circles under his eyes make him look older than his thirty years, and his hair that would normally be meticulously styled appears disheveled.

I put my hand on his shoulder and say, "It's okay, Cole. I understand."

He glances at me in the passenger seat and I smile

to assure him that everything is okay. Because the truth is, everything *is* okay. I know that Caitlyn has been having a difficult pregnancy and I sometimes wish I could be there to support Cole as he has done numerous times for me over the years.

"I should be the one apologizing for not being around to help," I say.

"What? Don't be ridiculous, Travis. You visit us any chance you get. I understand. We all do." He reaches up and taps my hand that's on his shoulder. "Plus, you can always just hop on another private jet." He smirks.

I grab my phone out of my pocket as I remember the unread text messages still waiting for replies. I've been so busy catching up with my brother that I almost forgot about them. I unlock the screen and a few dozen unread messages assault my eyes. I groan and Cole looks at me with worry in his eyes.

"What's wrong? Is everything okay?" He's looking back and forth between the road and me.

"Yeah, it's all good," I say reassuringly, trying to ease his concern. I show him my phone and he laughs. "It will take me forever to respond to all these texts."

I peruse each message to make sure that nothing is urgent and needs my immediate attention. They're mostly congratulatory messages and requests for more

Chapter Four

interviews. I make a mental note to call Aaliyah when I get home and ask her to take care of these interviews. I go through the notifications one by one until I reach the last message. My entire body tenses up in shock as I stare at the sender. I take a deep breath and steady my shaking hands as I read it.

Ash: *Congratulations, Travis!*

"We're here," Cole announces, bringing me out of my stupor.

"Huh?" I say in confusion, trying to gather myself. "Where are we?"

"We're here," he says worriedly. "Are you okay? You've been staring at your phone for the past fifteen minutes."

"Yes, I'm...I'm just a little tired I guess." I see Cole's eyes soften as if he's about to say something when the front door to the modern home where our parents live opens and grabs our attention.

I see Dad hurry in our direction. He kisses Cole's cheeks and gives him a big bear hug, just like he has done since we were little kids. As usual, Cole wipes his cheeks animatedly as he pretends to dislike the gesture. I've always admired my father for being expressive with his emotions and never hesitating to tell us how much he loves us every time we see each other.

"Where's Mom?" I ask. And as if my thoughts summon her existence, we see her waving her hands excitedly as she whips around the corner from the side yard, probably from tending her impeccably manicured garden.

"Here she is," Dad announces. She makes a beeline toward me and peppers me with kisses.

"Hi, Mom!" I snicker when she finally lets me go.

"I am so glad you're home. Let's get you boys inside."

"Actually, Mom, I can't stay long. I have to pick up Caitlyn's prescription from our pharmacy," Cole says.

Mom's face falls. "Oh sweetie, is she still having that awful nausea?"

"Yeah. We saw her ob-gyn yesterday and she gave her a new prescription." Mom comes around the SUV to give Cole a hug.

"Please let your dad and I know if you need us to watch the girls so you can focus on her and to give both of you a break."

"I might take you up on that offer. I'll mention it to Caitlyn."

After Cole says his goodbye, Mom, Dad and I make our way inside the house. We spend time catching up with each other, and after about an hour, I excuse myself to get some rest.

Chapter Four

I stare at my phone again and reread the text message from Ash that has been occupying my thoughts since I read it earlier. *Congratulations, Travis!* Those two words are the last thought on my mind when I finally succumb to sleep.

I open my eyes slowly as the weak sound of chatter wakes me from my nap. I easily recognize Mom and Dad's voices, and I can tell they have company. I try to listen to their faint voices, but I can't make out their conversation. However, when the other woman speaks, I find myself wondering who it could be. There's something remarkably familiar about the tone of her voice. It's soft and sweet like my mom's, but has a hint of confidence and assurance. I lay there for a few more minutes trying to figure out where I've heard that voice before, but I can't place it in my mind.

The light streaming through the window is noticeably dimmer than when I laid down earlier. I glance at my watch to learn that it's already six o'clock. The combination of jet lag and the four straight days of press conferences and TV appearances are finally catching up with me. No wonder I slept through most of the afternoon. Still feeling a little groggy, I force myself out of bed and head straight to the bathroom to freshen up and make sure I look presentable to my parents' guests.

I see a man and a woman, about my mom and dad's age, leaving while I'm descending the stairs. Mom sees me after she closes the door.

"There you are, honey! Did you get some rest?" she asks cheerily.

"I did, Mom. I can't believe I wasted the whole afternoon sleeping though."

Dad raises his arms from his sides, a big smile on his face. Not sure what's going on, I raise an eyebrow at him in confusion.

"You haven't given me a proper hug since you got here this afternoon," he says.

I roll my eyes and walk toward him, but it takes me by surprise when he grabs me and puts my head into a head lock, scuffing my hair. So typical of my dad.

"Who were those guests?" I inquire. "I heard you both talking to someone when I was upstairs."

"Oh, honey, did we wake you?" Mom apologizes.

"No, I was actually glad something woke me up," I assure her while giving her a side hug. "So, who was it?"

"Oh, it was the Kennedys. Do you remember Olivia and Preston?"

Do I remember? How could I forget? They're Ashton's parents and were almost like my second parents growing up. That's how I know her voice.

"Of course. How are they?"

Chapter Four

"They're doing very well. I mentioned that you were coming so they wanted to say hello."

"You should have woken me up, Mom."

"Did you know that—" She's interrupted by the ringing of her cellphone. "I'm sorry, sweetie, I have to take this call. It's the caterer for the party."

"What party?" I look at Dad as soon as Mom leaves the room to take the call.

"It's your mom's idea," Dad answers with a shrug.

Chapter Five
Travis

The past few days went by uneventfully, which is a welcome change of pace from the hectic few weeks since winning the Open. I spent much of yesterday catching up on unanswered emails and text messages from friends and colleagues, but there is one text in particular that I haven't been able to reply to. I can't seem to find the right words to respond to Ash. His message was so out of the blue that I'm not sure if he'd meant to send it to me. Was he expecting a response? Was he just being nice? Did he mean what he said? Was he really proud of me? And just like yesterday, I'm overthinking it again.

It's been four days since I received that text, and I'm quite sure I've missed the opportunity to reply. "Ugh," I groan, as I stare at the message for what seems

Chapter Five

like the hundredth time. He's going to think that I'm purposely ignoring his message. Therefore, before driving myself crazy, I call the one person who can give me the best advice for this situation.

"Do you miss me already? What did you do this time?" Aaliyah answers without skipping a beat.

"Don't flatter yourself. You are not that special. Besides, this is a personal call."

"Is it now?" she says in a tone laced with humor.

"How long is too long for responding to someone's text message?"

"Ten minutes. Thirty tops. Why?"

"Nothing in particular. I've been so caught up in being home that I've forgotten to respond to some of my messages." My lie is followed by the usual guilt associated with my dishonesty, especially with the one good friend I have. I know this makes me the worst friend on Earth, but I don't have any excuse besides the same lame one I've been using for the past few years.

"It's okay. That's what I'm here for. Send me their names and contacts and I'll make sure to spin something for you," she says, slipping seamlessly into agent extraordinaire mode.

"That's not necessary. I'll do it."

"When are you going to do it, Travis? If any of those messages are from the companies you endorse, you can't just ignore them." She pauses. "Besides, I'm your agent, this is literally what I'm here for."

"That's not the only reason you're here, and you know it." And it's the truth. Although our relationship started as an agent/talent relationship, we've developed a bond that I share with very few people.

"Travis, is everything okay?" she asks again.

"It's someone from my past," I admit, not being too specific.

"Oh. It always is. Well, just text her back. I'm sure she'll understand."

"Maybe," I sigh.

The assumption that it's a woman makes me sick to my stomach, and my fucking lying again only adds to the nausea. Guilt is starting to overcome my senses, so I need to end this call before Aaliyah notices my agitation.

"I'd better go. I still have to get ready for the party tonight." I hang up without hearing her response.

I glance out the window of my childhood bedroom to see the party is underway. The lights strung above the meticulously cut lawn gives the evening a magical feel. Soft jazz music is playing in the background, while the caterer's team, all dressed in white shirts and black ties, walk around offering gourmet appetizers and refilling glasses of wine.

Chapter Five

Everyone is dressed impeccably. When my mom informed me about the party, she hadn't mentioned the size of the crowd was going be this large. There must be at least a hundred people here, and I can count on one hand who I recognize. Well, maybe that's an exaggeration, but aside from my immediate family and close friends, the rest are strangers.

A small tap on the partially open door catches my attention, and I see my dad coming in before I have a chance to answer.

"You don't plan to hide in here all night, do you?" he asks, looking elegant in his formal wear.

"Do you think they'll notice?"

"Listen, I know your mom said she was hosting a small shindig with family and close friends, but as usual, she got carried away. She's just proud of you." He smiles apologetically.

"I know, Dad. I'll be out there soon. By the way, you look great."

As I make my way out of the house to join the party, I'm immediately stopped by several people congratulating me on my big win. I engage in several short conversations and excuse myself after a few minutes with each person, politely moving along to the next guest.

The next thirty minutes go like that and finally I'm able to catch the eye of a server. This night calls for some alcohol. I grab the first glass of wine he offers, give my quick thanks, and walk toward the corner of the lawn overlooking the city to join my parents and their friends.

As I get closer to them, I recognize the couple they're talking to. They see me walking toward them and they both give me the sweetest smile.

"Olivia, Preston! It is so nice to see you!" I extend my hand out to Mr. and Mrs. Kennedy.

"Travis! It's been so long!" Olivia waves my hand away to pull me in and give me a hug, followed by a kiss on the cheek. As soon as she releases me, Preston follows suit.

"Travis, we are so proud of you," Preston says.
The dread that I'm feeling suddenly washes away in their presence. They've known me since I was a ten-year-old running around like a hellion in their house with Ash.

"Thank you, Preston. I'm sorry it's been so long. My schedule has been hectic," I say, stopping myself from telling another lie.

"It's okay, sweetheart. We understand. No need to apologize!" And because she knows me so well, Olivia assures me that she means what she says.

"Thank you."

I spend a good amount of time reconnecting with the Kennedys. I learn that Olivia is planning on taking a

Chapter Five

sabbatical from work to slow down a bit and spend more time with her family. Preston has also stepped down from his role as CEO of one of the leading pharmaceutical companies that specializes in pediatric diabetes.

However, there is one subject they seem to avoid discussing—Ash. I'm not sure if it's on purpose, but I can't think of any reason why they wouldn't mention him. They know we were best friends and wouldn't know anything else about my relationship with him. Hell, I don't think anyone does.

"Have you seen Ashton since you arrived?" Olivia finally asks.

"Ash? No, why?" I say, sounding defensive for no reason. Do they know? Did Ash tell them? Who else did he tell?

"I figured that since you're both in Seattle and were two peas in a pod, you would have connected by now."

Why the sudden shift to him? Is she fishing for something or am I being paranoid? Has Ash updated his folks? I need another drink, preferably one stiffer than wine.

"Oh, no, I haven't seen him. How long is he going to be in town?" I ask, hoping for more details.

"Travis, he started his residency in Seattle two months ago. You knew that, right?"

My eyes shoot toward Olivia, unsure if I heard her correctly. "Ash is back in Seattle?"

I hear my mom as she comes up behind me. "Yes, I just had lunch with him a couple of weeks ago. I forgot to mention it when you arrived. I invited him tonight, by the way."

"Invited who?" I ask.

"Ashton, of course! Are you okay, Travis? Weren't you and Olivia just speaking about him?"

"What did he say? Is he coming?" I ask, holding my breath for an answer.

"He said he'll try his best," Olivia informs me.

My mom asks me to meet some of the guests who just arrived to see me, but my attention is somewhere else. Ash is back in Seattle and there's a chance he will be here. Just the thought of seeing him tonight makes my heart race. Will he come? What if he doesn't? Will I be disappointed?

I run myself haggard watching every newcomer join the party, and after more time passes and there is still no sign of Ash, I'm convinced that he won't be here. With my concentration declining, I make an excuse to go to the bathroom to have a moment to myself and gather my composure. I tell my mind not to be hopeful, but I am. I tell my spirit that I won't be depleted, but I am. I tell my heart that I won't be disappointed, but I am. Because even though I am surrounded by a sea of people, the one I long to see is the one who may not come. Resolved, I go inside the house to get away from the crowd.

Chapter Five

"Trav?" I hear someone call my name as I make my way upstairs. The hairs on the back of my neck stand up and goosebumps spontaneously appear all over my body as a wave of excitement and nervousness occupies all my senses.

I know that voice, I recognize that voice. And only one person calls me by that nickname.

"Ash?" I whisper as I turn to find the source of the voice.

There he is, standing by the doorway, biting his lower lip. The only thing I manage to do is stare.

Chapter Six
Ashton

It's like I'm frozen in time. Everything around me ceases to exist the moment Travis' eyes lock with mine. The echoes of chatter inside the house diminish while the party's commotion fades into the background. In an instant, the room turns quiet to the point where all I can hear is the sound of Travis' footsteps as he descends the staircase.

Neither one of us dares to look away and the smaller the distance between us becomes, the more I grow aware of all the emotions this reunion brings to the surface. Little by little, I summon all my will power to patch the gaping hole threatening to create an avalanche of unwanted emotions from leaking out. Without any success, I stay still, fearing that the tiniest movement will send me into shambles. Both figuratively and literally.

Chapter Six

The initial shock that I saw on his face is replaced with a probing stare, an unreadable stare. His eyes are searching for something. For what, I don't know.

I had been standing by the doorway for a few minutes, trying to find the courage to join the rest of the party, when I saw him make a beeline upstairs. I don't know what possessed me to yell out his name, his nickname no less, but I knew I had to or I would lose the opportunity to do what I had come here for. I'd thought I would make a quick appearance, find Travis, congratulate him on his win, and be on my merry way. Now that we are inches apart, that's when my senses decide to go haywire. The familiar scent of Travis' favorite cologne goes for the kill and takes me back to the last time we saw each other. The day he said goodbye. Vividly, I can still recall that day. It was the darkest day of my young life. The day that I try hard to suppress. But just like a shadow, the past can be behind you, but it never goes away.

***

Six years earlier

Travis looked like he had ants crawling under his skin as he paced my room. The redness of his eyes and the dark shadows around them made him look tired. What would normally be a clean-shaven face was peppered with a few days' worth of facial hair. One of his hands was tucked in the back pocket of his jeans as the other one combed through his hair.

Sitting on the edge of the bed, I braced for what was about to come.

Travis had been distant the past couple of weeks and even when he was around, it felt like his mind was somewhere else. I initially chalked it up to the pressure of playing for the NCAA Tennis Championship that month, but it lingered even after he and his team had won the tournament. I asked him on multiple occasions if he was okay and his answer was always a quick *yes*.

As the days went by, he became even more distant. There were times when I saw him looking at me and when he smiled, it felt empty. His behavior became worse after his second meeting with the pro tennis coach, Charlie Sullivan. He was never unkind or rude toward me because I knew he didn't have it in him to be hurtful, but the Travis I knew was gone. Where? I didn't know.

I hadn't seen him in three days when I received a text from him wanting to talk. I didn't have a lot of experience with relationships and Travis was the only person I had been with romantically, but even I knew that text spelled trouble with a capital T.

I spent countless time going over all the events that

Chapter Six

had happened that could have brought this up, but the answer never came. I didn't think that he found someone else because no one knew he was gay but me. Whatever his reason was for this behavior, I was certain that I knew where this conversation was headed.

He took another deep breath as he tried to calm his shaking hands and after watching the scene unfold over and over again like a skipping record, I finally had enough. Impatiently, I stood up and blocked his movement, preventing him from going anywhere. He was looking at everything but me, so I lightly grabbed his chin to turn it my direction. Once I finally had his attention, I slid my hand from his chin down his neck and to his chest. I let my hand rest there, where I felt his heart beating.

"Just say it," I urged him. "You clearly have something to say, so just cut to the chase and say it."

Pain was written all over his face, draining it of color. His heavy breathing became the only audible sound in the room, making the tension even higher. I saw a war being fought in his head, but he managed to say in almost a whisper, "I don't know how to do this."

"Do what, Travis?" Another silence met my question. "Goddamn it, Travis. Just say it! I never pegged you as a coward." That seemed to get to him, just like I knew it would.

"I can't do this anymore."

"You can't or you won't?" My voice broke as I realized what was happening. He was ending us.

"Please, don't make this harder."

"Harder for who?" I pushed him and he let me. Uncontrollable tears flowed, pleading for him to take his words back. "Why?" I continued to ask when he didn't answer my question. "What are you afraid of?" My voice was borderline begging.

"I just can't. I'm sorry," he said as he wiped his tears with his hand while the other searched his pocket for his car keys.

"Travis, look at me. Please!" I tried to grab him, but I slipped as he was leaving, which caused me to land on my knee. Travis looked back and debated whether to help me stand up, but instead he just looked away, avoiding my pleading eyes.

"I have to go. I'm so sorry, Ash."

"Travis! Wait, don't go. Please stay. Please! I love you!"

I didn't know how long I stayed kneeling on the floor but when my body started aching from being in that position, I laid back and all I could do was stare at the empty space, hoping Travis would have a change of heart and come back. Rolling to my side, I drew my knees up to my chest for comfort as more hours passed and the dawn made way to a new day.

Chapter Six

***

"Hi," I finally manage to say, as I return from my quick trip down memory lane. He's still looking at me as if he's seen a ghost. I wait for a second and add, "Trying to escape your own party?"

My attempt to lighten the mood puts him at ease. His shoulders relax and his facial expression softens. The look of shock is replaced with his usual lop-sided grin and I can't help but notice how much he's changed physically since I last saw him six years ago. I've seen him play on television, but seeing him in person and this close is way different than I have imagined.

He's now sporting facial hair groomed to outline his square jaw, and because of years of playing outdoors, his tan complexion gives his face a glow that accentuates his hazel eyes. My gaze travels down to his impressive broad shoulders. He's still the same height but with a bigger build.

The well-fitting suit that he's wearing outlines the muscular physique from the intense training he routinely does to stay in shape. As my watchful eyes return to his face, his grin is even wider, and that's when I realize what I've been doing. I'm checking him out. I can't believe I'm shamelessly checking him out. I feel my body warming up and I can only imagine the flush of red creeping across my face.

"Dr. Ashton Kennedy, it's not polite to stare," he teases as he closes the distance between us. We're now standing just inches apart and his scent fills up the tiny space.

"So, are you ditching your own party?" I repeat.

"Of course not, I'm just going to take a quick break. I don't suppose you want to join me?"

"What? I just got here," I say, taken aback by his offer.

"So?"

"I'll see you outside," I say, shaking my head, and then I turn around and walk out to the garden. The truth is, I need to get away to calm myself because if I don't, I might embarrass myself even more and I've been here for less than an hour.

I spot Mr. and Mrs. Montgomery right away and walk toward them to make my presence known. "Great party, Emily and Arthur!" I say.

"Oh, Ashton, you made it," Mrs. Montgomery squeals, cupping her hands to her chest excitedly.

"I'm sorry I'm late. I had a last-minute surgery added to my schedule today."

"No worries, sweetheart. I'm glad you could make it."

"Me too." I look around to survey the impressive venue. The Montgomerys really know how to throw a party. The garden is illuminated by hundreds of mini lanterns hanging across the whole span of the yard, while dozens of bistro tables covered with white linen surround the dance floor in the center.

Arthur and Emily excuse themselves as more guests arrive. I look for my parents to make sure that they see me, since they've been bugging me to come the past few days. It doesn't take me long to spot them having a conversation with a group of three other couples. As if he can sense my presence, my dad glances my direction and I wave. He whispers something to my mom, presumably to let her know I've arrived, and they wave at me to join them, so I do.

I spend the next few minutes listening to my mom brag about me to her friends. Politely, I answer their questions about my training and what I do for fun while combing the crowd for Travis.

More of my parents' friends join our circle and I start to feel overwhelmed by all the people and the attention being thrown my way. This should have made me feel welcome, but it makes me feel alone. It's unsettling to feel lonely in a room full of people, most of whom are family and friends.

I excuse myself the moment I find an available exit from the series of questions that have started to sound like an interrogation. I want to find a place where I can be alone for a while, but the entire garden is filled with people dancing and talking. I know this place like the back of my hand, so I make my way down to the corner where I can find a safe harbor from this sea of people.

I follow the graveled path leading to a lower smaller garden that Travis and I used to hide in when we were kids. I'm greeted by the scent of leftover summer honeysuckle that hangs from a trellis in the garden. I walk to the wooden bench that overlooks the city, and sit and marvel at the spectacular view in front of me.

"I knew I'd find you here," a voice says, interrupting the silence.

Not just any voice, but Travis' voice.

Chapter Seven
Travis

There are very few things in life that render me surprised, but seeing Ashton today is at the top of that list. After the way I treated him six years ago, I wouldn't have been surprised if he didn't show up. But here we are, and I'm now standing face-to-face with Ash after six long years.

I notice how different he looks. He actually looks better, if that's possible. He's a bit leaner now, with a good twenty pounds of muscle in all the right places, which makes his clothes fit better than before. His dark-brown hair is longer, with a trendier cut, making him look even sexier. And with those beautiful baby blues behind his black-framed glasses, I'm a goner.

I have always been physically and sexually attracted to Ash, and no one does it for me the way he does. Not that I have the luxury to look around, since my closet is deeper than any of the seven seas.

When he chooses not to follow me upstairs, I return to my room and stay cooped up there. Being the coward that I am, I watch him from my bedroom window as he interacts with my parents, his parents, and their group of friends. Even from a distance, his demeanor begins to change. His posture tenses and he puts his hand behind his neck to relieve the pressure, and that's how I know he's stressed. A few minutes pass and he leaves the crowd. That's when I decide to head out.

I follow Ash when he makes his way to the part of the garden not known to a lot of people. The moment I see him heading in that direction, I know he's going to our secret spot.

Ash is lost in his thoughts to the point that he doesn't realize my presence. I hesitate to say something, not truly aware of what I want to say.

What do you say to someone whose heart you broke? *Hi! Do you remember me? The coward who chose to lie to the world and hide who I really was for my career over the one person who didn't want me to be anything other than myself? The asshole who chose his ambition over the person who genuinely loved me and made me the happiest?*

I should walk away and give him space, but the desire to know if I'd completely broken him overwhelms me.

Chapter Seven

"I knew I'd find you here."

His body tenses up and what I wouldn't give to see his eyes, the one part of him that always gives him away. "What are you doing here?" Ash says without turning around.

I'm taken aback by the tone of his voice. Gone is the sweet boy I remember. Guilt that I'm the reason why that version of Ash is gone makes me physically ill. When I don't answer, he turns around and looks at me, urging me to respond. He must have noticed my distress because I see his features soften.

"Are you okay?" he asks. I chuckle at that. This has to be the worst punishment ever. Here I am, sick to my stomach for all the horrible things I've done to him, and here he is, asking if I'm okay.

"Trav, are you okay?" he repeats. That he uses my nickname somewhat eases the guilt that is overwhelming me, making me snicker just a bit. "What's so funny?" he continues, sounding irritated.

"Nothing, I'm fine. I just...never mind," I reply lamely.

"What are you doing here? You're missing your party," he says dryly.

"They won't even notice I'm gone."

"Really? You think they won't notice? Isn't this party for you and your victory?"

"Nope. I bet you half of the people don't even know

what the party is about," I tease, trying to defuse the tension between us.

"There's a big banner that says *Congratulations Travis* when you enter the garden. It's literally a reminder of what this evening is about."

"There is? I hadn't noticed." I walk toward him, and when I'm standing next to him, I continue. "Where is this sign you speak of?" I'm still trying hard to lighten the mood.

"You're kidding, right?"

"What?" I add innocently.

Clearly not understanding my failed attempt at humor, Ash attempts to leave. I grab his arm to pull him back to me, but to my surprise he yanks it out of my grasp aggressively and looks at me with fury.

"I'm sorry," I say, raising my hands up in surrender.
"Don't touch me! Don't you dare touch me!" he says in a low but firm voice, pointing his finger at me.

All I am able to say is a repeated, "I'm sorry."

"Sorry about what?" His question is challenging, and I have a feeling that he's not only asking about what happened minutes ago, but also about what I did six years ago. I don't say anything. I can make up excuses and lies to get me out of this situation, but because I've promised myself that I will never lie to him, I sit on the bench and don't say anything.

"That's what I fucking thought. Maybe you should

just go now and join your party. Isn't this what you've always wanted? Or is it too small for you?" he says as he walks away.

Ash's words are like daggers aimed at a perfect target, and because what he said is true, I decide to let him disappear into the crowd.

If only I could tell him what I really want.

Chapter Eight
Ashton

I'm being a jerk and I know it. But what am I supposed to do? Hold his hand, sing *Kumbaya*, and just forget all the pain and suffering he'd put me through?

Not happening.

I practically run away from him to stop myself from apologizing for what I said. After seeing the hurt in his eyes, my self-control lets me summon all my memories of the past and helps me stand my ground. My whole body is trembling, and I feel like vomiting. My stomach has been in knots since I arrived, and it'll take days to untie them all. I've been here less than an hour and I'm spiraling out of control.

This evening is turning out to be more than I can handle. The well-rehearsed plan I've prepared is

Chapter Eight

nothing but trash now. And the longer I stay here, the more I might reveal how rattled I am by Travis' presence.

My quick escape from where I left Travis doesn't go unnoticed. Halfway across the dance floor, I hear my mom calling my name. I think about ignoring her for a split second, but I know better. One of my mother's strengths—or weaknesses, depending on who you ask—is her perseverance and willingness to always get what she wants, no matter the cost. I guess that's one of the reasons why she's a successful surgeon.

My relationship with my mom these past few years has been interesting to say the least. There's no doubting the love we have for each other, but there is a certain level of animosity and lingering tension between us whenever we're alone. My dad serves as a buffer whenever I visit, and without him around, I don't know how this interaction will go.

Our relationship has been like this since before I left for college.

Chapter Nine
Ashton

Eight years ago

"Did we get a package from Stanford?" I asked Dad as he entered the house from picking up our mail one spring Saturday morning.

I had been on edge for days, knowing this was the week when letters from colleges and universities were being sent. I'd received two acceptance letters from my safe schools, but I'd been hoping to get something from Stanford, my first choice, since both of my parents were active alumni. But aside from my family's history with the university, I knew that they had one of the best pre-med programs and medical schools in the country.

I'd done everything I possibly could to improve my application. I volunteered at the local shelter

Chapter Nine

and assisted doctors and nurses providing care for homeless teens. I even signed up for all the extracurricular activities that our high school offered, while maintaining a perfect 4.0 GPA. Initially, I did all this to make my application competitive, but what I didn't realize was how much I enjoyed all that, to the point that I made it a commitment to lend my time to help those who were less fortunate than I.

"Nothing yet, son. Maybe tomorrow," Dad said. He didn't seem worried, but he didn't sound convincing either.

"Yeah, maybe tomorrow," I said brightly, overcompensating for his lack of enthusiasm.

"Are you heading out?"

"Yes, Travis has some good news that he'd like to share with me. I'm meeting him at the tennis academy."

"Do you think he'll tell you which school he's decided to play for?" Dad asked cheerfully. I can't blame him from being this excited, really. My parents had followed Travis' matches since he'd shown potential. At first, I thought they went because of me, but I since realized how much they cared for him. I sometimes wished I could tell them that he was more than my best friend, but I knew the rules. I couldn't do that until Travis was ready. I hoped it would be soon.

"I think so. I'll definitely let you know."

Before I was able to get out of the house, my mom arrived.

"Anything from Stanford today?" she asked as she came inside after working two straight days at the hospital. Being a trauma surgeon required her to be on call one week every other month, and these past couple of days had been unusually busy, according to my dad when she missed dinner the last few nights.

"Nothing yet. Maybe tomorrow," I said hopefully, my optimism not fading.

I didn't miss the look that my mom gave my dad as I kissed both of them goodbye. I couldn't really figure it out, but my excitement to see Travis was stronger than my will to work out what the suspicious look meant.

It took ten minutes to get to the tennis academy, and because my parents belonged to the country club it's in, I was able to park in the members-only parking lot.

It didn't take me long to find Travis, and it looked like he was having a serious conversation with his coach. I saw him shaking his head. I waited in the car for a few more minutes until his coach left and he was alone. He looked defeated and I quickly got out of the car to make sure he was alright.

The moment Travis saw me his whole aura changed. Gone was the worried look, replaced by pure joy at seeing me.

"Is everything okay?" I asked when I got to him. He gave me a quick hug, and to my surprise gave my ass a little tap too.

Chapter Nine

"It is now that you're here. What took you so long?"

"I got here about ten minutes ago, but I saw you talking to your coach and I didn't want to interrupt. He already views me as a distraction," I said.

"Don't mind him. He's just an ass. I can't wait until I go to college, so I don't have to put up with him."

"Is that why you asked me to come here? Which school did you choose?" I asked impatiently.

"Well, yes and no," he smiled.

"What do you mean? It's either yes or no, so what is it?"

"You are so bossy!" he protested but the look on his face said he wasn't bothered.

"You like it when I'm bossy."

"That I do. As long as I'm the boss of you-know-where." He winked.

"So? Which school?" I asked again.

"Have you heard from Stanford?" he asked.

"Nothing this morning, but hopefully I will this week. What does it have to do with you?"

"So far you've only heard from UCLA and University of Washington, yeah?" he continued to question.

"Yes, you know I'd tell you if I received more. And if you answer my questions with more questions, I'm leaving."

"Okay, okay. Stanford, UCLA, and Florida want me," Travis finally admitted.

"Oh my goodness, Trav! That's awesome. So where are you going to go?"

"I asked if I could give them my answer next week, because I was hoping to know first if you were going to Stanford, and they agreed."

"Trav, you don't have to do that. What if they change their minds?"

"They won't, they've seen me play," he said. His confidence was one of the qualities I admired most about him. "Besides, I don't want to go anywhere without you."

My heart swelled after that statement, because it showed that he cared. His inability to come out brought some insecurities, so hearing him say that assured me that he loved me.

"Trav?" I asked warily.

"Yeah?" he said, giving me all of his attention.

"What if I don't get into Stanford?"

"Ash, you're the smartest kid in our school. Of course you'll get in"

"But what if I don't? I know how much you love the athletic program at Stanford. That's why it's your first choice."

"My first choice is to go where you go."

"Do you think you'll come out in college? I hear that a lot of teens wait until they're out of high school to come out."

Chapter Nine

"I don't know, maybe," Travis said guardedly.

We spent the next hour hanging out until it was time for us to go. On my drive home, I couldn't help but wonder why Travis got so tense and uneasy whenever the topic of coming out came up. His parents were like mine; they were supportive and loving, especially toward their two boys. They had treated me with love and respect when I had come out, so I wasn't sure what the hesitation was about.

My mom and dad were waiting for me in the living room when I got home. They were both sitting on leather chairs by the fireplace, and when they asked me to sit down on the sofa opposite them, my curiosity grew.

"What's going on? Who died?" I said and my dad chuckled from the question.

"Oh, Ash, sweetie, no one." Mom waved me off. "We just want to give you the great news."

"What is it?"

"You're going to Stanford!" Mom proudly announced.

"Oh my god! Are you sure? Dad, did you miss the letter?" I turned to him, unable to hide my excitement. He just looked at Mom and she continued.

"No, I made a call to one of my friends who happens to be the chair of the college acceptance committee, and let's just say we had a very long chat."

"Please say more. Did she tell you that I was accepted, and the letter is on its way?"

"No, she couldn't tell me that."

"Did she...tell you that I wasn't accepted?" I asked, slightly confused by the direction of the conversation.

"She didn't tell me that either."

"Then, how did I get in?" Silence.

"Mom, what have you done?" I asked her as the realization of what had happened became clear.

"Ashton, honey, this is great news."

"Not this way, Mom. I've spent my entire high school years making sure I do everything I can to get there on my own. I want to get accepted on my own merit. Not because my big-shot mommy did it for me."

"What's the big deal?" she asked, clearly missing my point.

"This is a big deal for me. You always do this when you don't get your way. Why can't you just believe that I'm capable of doing things on my own? Don't you think I'm good enough? Honestly, am I good enough for you, Mom?" The tears that I'd been holding in started flowing and I ran up to my room, ignoring my parents calling after me.

I spent the weekend locked in my room and only came out in the middle of the night when everyone was asleep so I could eat. I was still in disbelief that my mom had used her connections to get me into Stanford.

Chapter Nine

When Monday finally arrived, I had classes all morning, then spent the rest of the day hanging out with friends, and I watched Travis practice. The rest of that week went basically the same.

On Friday when I got home, my dad handed me a letter from Stanford University. I held the letter in my hand, staring at the return address. I was afraid to open it, but went ahead anyways.

Dear Ashton Kennedy, Congratulations! It is with great pleasure that I offer you admission to the University of Stanford Class of 2015.

After reading the first sentence, I shook my head in disbelief.

"So?" Dad asked.

"I got accepted."

"Then why the sad face?"

"I only got accepted because of Mom and you know it!" I yelled. I felt guilty for raising my voice.

"Son, your mom only called a week ago, this letter couldn't have come from that. You did it! You got accepted because of all your hard work."

"I guess I'll never know. I'm tired, Dad, I'm going upstairs."

"Ash..."

"I'm sorry. I can't right now."

The moment I got to my bedroom, there was only one person that I wanted to talk to, and I wished that

Travis was actually there right next to me. My entire body was trembling in anger as I dialed his number and he picked up after one ring.

"So, any news from Stanford?" he pressed.

"I got the letter today," I started, unable to finish my answer due to the lump in my throat. It was filled with the disappointment that I might never know whether I was good enough to get into the school of my choice. "I didn't get it," I lied, knowing that I had made my choice not to attend. "But you should go. You can't—"

"It's their loss. I'm not going either," Travis said, interrupting me.

"Trav, this is serious. You can't just change your future because I'm not good enough to get in."

"Stop saying that. So, what are you going to do now? You want me to come over?" As much as I wanted him here, I just needed to be alone. "I've decided on UCLA," I said.

"Then we're both going to be Bruins. What are bruins?" he asked, trying to cheer me up and lighten the mood.

"I guess we'll find out."

Chapter Ten
Travis

My interaction with Ash, just minutes ago, should have deterred me from running after him. I should've just let him go and let him be on his way and forget this evening ever happened. But the truth is, I haven't been able to completely detach from Ash. Not then, and I don't think I will be able to now. There was never a time within the past six years that I didn't think of him, when I didn't want to share all my wins with him, and above all, he was the one I wanted to console me when I suffered a loss.

The will to know if this new Ash is the cold and tough guy I met today is stronger than the need to take my next breath. I refuse to believe the Ash I know is gone. I need to know that somewhere inside this new tough persona still lies my Ash.

I find him in the middle of the dance floor, looking lost in thought as his mom approaches him.

"Ash! Ash!" I hear Olivia Kennedy yell his name, and that brings him out of whatever trance he's in.

"I'm looking for Emily and Arthur to say my goodbye. I have an early day tomorrow," I hear Ash respond.

"Oh. Have you at least congratulated Travis?" Mrs. Kennedy says as I get closer to where they are standing.

"I saw him earlier and—" Ash's words are cut off when Olivia spots me.

"There he is!" she exclaims.

Ash turns to face me, not realizing I'm right behind him. This startles him and he loses his balance. I instinctively reach out and grab his arm to steady him, and a zap of electricity goes haywire through my body. Our faces are inches apart and the warmth of his breath fans my lips oh so delicately that I momentarily forget why I'm here. His eyes gaze at my lips and I see his Adam's apple move up and down as he swallows, causing his breath to hitch.

"Travis, what a great party!" I'm thankful for Olivia's interruption that breaks the spell we're under. Ash moves a couple of steps backward to give us some needed space. Which I guess is a good thing, as I don't know what I would have done had we stayed that close for another minute.

"I'm glad you're enjoying yourself. Can I borrow Ash

Chapter Ten

for a minute?" I ask Olivia.

"Of course, you two have a lot to catch up on," she says, and turns to rejoin her group of friends.

"Can we talk?" I ask when we're alone.

"Okay, so talk."

"Can we go in the house, please?"

"This better be quick," he declares impatiently.

"I promise."

"Don't use words you don't understand."

I don't falter this time and I'm even more determined to find out, once and for all, where my Ash has gone.

We're stopped on our way inside by Cole and his very pregnant wife, Caitlyn. I didn't expect him to make it to the party, and to have him here with Caitlyn is more than I can ask for.

"Caitlyn, Cole, how are you guys?" Ash greets them cheerily and gives them both a hug. He focuses his attention on Caitlyn. "It's so nice to see you out. How are you feeling?"

"I feel so much better. I mentioned your recommendation to my doctor and after taking those meds for a couple of days, I feel like myself again. Thank you again, Ash," she says, and gives him a kiss on his cheek.

"Of course. If you ever need anything, just call."

The way Ash interacts with my brother and Caitlyn catches me off guard. This is the Ash I used to know.

Relief washes over me knowing that he's still like his old self, but I'm also sad that I might never again be the recipient of that version of him. Instead, all I might get is the one I deserve.

"Congrats, Travis! We're so proud of you," Caitlyn says and also kisses me on my cheek. Cole follows suit and gives me a hug.

"Thank you. I'm glad you're feeling better."

"Me too, thanks to your buddy, Ash," she teases, giving Ash another side hug. "You could always do obstetrics if the whole sports medicine thing doesn't work out."

Cole and Caitlyn excuse themselves to find Mom and get something to eat. Her last statement makes me curious. Why did Ash choose sports medicine? I stand in silence, watching them join the party, and when I finally make myself speak, I ask, "Sports medicine? Your residency is in sports medicine?"

This revelation shouldn't have shocked me, but the need to know why he has chosen this field is something I am dying to find out.

"Yes. What about it?" He isn't as brash as earlier, but every time he looks at me, it's with a quick glance. I wonder if he knows that his eyes always give his true feelings away.

"Nothing...I was just curious," I say, and my answer is met with a shrug.

Chapter Ten

"Where do you want to talk?"

"Let's go in my parents' office."

"Lead the way," Ash says, gesturing for me to go in front of him.

We walk in silence; there are so many things I want to say and questions I want to ask him. I know I will have to initiate all the talking in order to get an actual conversation going with him.

"So?" he asks once we're inside the office and I close the door.

This is as far as my plan goes and now that I have Ash's attention, I don't know where and how to begin. One thing I know for sure, I have no excuses. I search for the perfect opening and when nothing comes, Ash surprises me by starting instead.

"I'm sorry about earlier. That was unkind and you didn't deserve that." For the first time today, he finally looks at me, his eyes a bit softer than the fiery ones from earlier.

"I should be the one apologizing. And I don't mean just for today, but for all of it. I'm not going to give you any excuses because you deserve better than that."

"Travis, we don't have to do this."

"Just let me finish, please," I appeal.

"Okay."

"I'm sorry for leading you on for as long as I did. I was being selfish. I was only thinking about me and I didn't consider how it would affect you." It feels good to finally be able to say that. The liberation that comes from telling him the first part of my story urges me to keep going. "I'm so sorry I hurt you."

The tears that I've been fighting so hard feel like they have a mind of their own and I let them fall. "I wish I could say that I've learned and that I've finally grown some balls to do what you've always wanted me to do. But I'm stuck in the well of my own lies." Feeling like I'm exhausting all of my energy, I sit down on the edge of the wooden desk, steadying myself with my palms. I let my head fall to my chest because I cannot bear the look Ash is giving me.

Ash walks over, sits next to me and starts rubbing circles on my back. The affectionate move is meant to soothe me, but it only makes my feelings worse.

I stand in a hurry and go to the other side of the room. "Don't pity me. Don't fucking pity me. I want you to be angry. Be mad! Tell me that I am the worst person you've ever met. That being with me was a mistake. Anything. But don't fucking pity me. Not you."

I look up at him and find he is studying me. His gaze is piercing a hole in my soul, and there's nothing I want more than to run and hide. One stray tear falls on his left cheek and he moves to wipe it off before it lands on his chest.

"I don't pity you. I will never understand your fear,

Chapter Ten

but I don't pity you." After a long exhale, Ash continues. "Travis, I was angry, I was mad, but that was six years ago. You gave me no choice but to move on. What did you expect me to do?"

"I don't know what I expected you to do," I admit. "But before today, I wasn't sure if I would ever see you again. And now, standing here, I'm more confused by my emotions than ever."

"Travis, I can't do this with you anymore. We're not teenagers. We've both grown up. After five minutes of this, I can clearly see you haven't changed one bit."

"So, what? There's nothing left? Not even a chance for friendship?"

"Trav, you and I both know we can't just be friends. Let's at least be honest about that."

"You're not even willing to try?" I ask. "Maybe give me a chance to be your friend?"

"I don't know if that's a good idea, Travis."

"Please, just try, give me a chance," I beg in earnest.

Ash sits there, saying nothing. He's about to speak when a small knock on the door grabs our attention. The look of relief on his face after hearing the knock makes my curiosity grow higher, and I want to curse whoever is on the other side of the door.

"Travis, we need you out here. Your mom wants you to cut the cake," my dad calls out.

"I'll be out in a minute, Dad."

"Okay. Just hurry."

"And you said they wouldn't notice you were gone," Ash says sarcastically.

A beeping sound comes out of Ash's pocket. He lightly shakes his head as he reads his pager.

"This is the hospital. I have to go."

"Is everything okay?" I ask.

"Yes. I'm on call tonight and they have some questions. Will you let your mom and dad know I had to go?"

"Yeah, of course. Can I see you again?"

"Travis, I don't know," Ash answers, scratching his head.

"I just want to talk with you some more."

I see him debating what to do, but he eventually says, "Okay."

"How about dinner tomorrow? I'll text you the details." I'm sure I sound way too hopeful.

"I don't think so. How about tomorrow for brunch?"

"Fine."

"Give me your phone," he orders. Confused by the request, I hand him my cell and he begins entering my password without skipping a beat.

"Wait, you still know my password?" I ask.

"Yes, because I know you're too lazy to learn a new one. Seriously, Trav, you should change your password."

"Hey, that's not true," I protest as he starts typing.

Chapter Ten

He pauses for a moment. "What?" I ask.
"You have the same number?"
"Of course I do. What made you think I wouldn't?"
"I texted you and you never responded so I figured..."
"Yeah, about that...I'm sorry."
"Not important. I really have to go."

He leaves in a hurry and I shout out, "See you tomorrow."

With a new sense of purpose, I begin to plan. I will win my Ash back if it's the last thing I do.

I stay there for a moment, composing myself, then join the rest of the party.

Chapter Eleven
Ashton

Evidence-based decision-making has been my main mantra since the first day of medical school. I study facts and their correlations with current situations to analyze possible outcomes before making a hypothesis. I rely on science and proof to influence most of my day-to-day actions, and they've rescued me from some unpleasant situations in the past.

However, that principle went out the window the moment I agreed to meet Travis this morning. In fact, that rule has been nonexistent since the second I laid eyes on the tall, charming, broad-shouldered and sinfully handsome man with a wicked smile.

I'm no Clark Kent, but if I were Superman, Travis' smile would be my kryptonite.

The old Travis I knew from six years ago would not hold a candle to the new and improved version today.

Nope, not even close. The way Travis 2.0 carries himself and how his muscles move when he walks exudes confidence that would make any model envious. His deep voice with a hint of seduction is enough to make even a celibate monk reconsider his vow.

But what remains the same is his fear of being true to himself. The part of him that he battles and hides in the darkest part of his closet. I was ready to put him behind me, in my past where he can no longer hurt me, but his admission about where his life is heading and his plea to resume our friendship makes him hard to resist. My skepticism about Travis and I being friends is stronger in the light of day, and I still believe it's not the best idea. But I promised I would try.

My shift last night was uneventful, even though I had received a page while at the party, which was unfortunate because that gave me a lot of time to think and rethink about everything he'd said. His unexpected apology is something that has been heavy on my mind since the moment I left, and I was thankful that we were interrupted because I didn't know how much of it I could have handled, especially when he broke down and thought that I pitied him.

I don't pity him. I really don't. I just don't understand his fear of coming out. What is he so afraid of? Is he really going to spend the rest of his life hiding? What about his happiness?

I made a conscious decision last night that I will hear him out and try to be a friend, because even after all is said and done, I want to be his friend.

Knowing that parking will be an issue, I purposely arrive thirty minutes earlier than planned at Casa Italiana, an Italian bistro that serves some of the finest frittatas and crostatas in town. From the outside, there's nothing special about the place. Definitely not its location among the group of nondescript buildings in the slowest part of the city. But what it lacks in presentation, it makes up for in flavors. I think that's the reason why I love this place so much. No pretense; all quality.

The street is buzzing with activity, which is odd considering the time of day. All the street parking within four blocks is taken, so I keep driving around. After circling the block a couple of times, searching for a place to park, I see a car leaving and immediately take the spot.

I glance in the rear-view mirror to make sure my hair is in the right place, even though I'd already spent an exorbitant amount of time fixing it before I left the house. And I didn't spend time on just my hair—looking for an outfit was an event. I rummaged through my wardrobe to find something other than jeans, a UCLA sweatshirt, or scrubs. The silliness of it all should have bothered me, but the excitement **makes**

Chapter Eleven

me feel like I'm going out on a first date. Which is stupid in itself, because this is not a date, and even if it were, it would not be my first with Travis.

The idea that I'm going out for brunch with one of the most popular athletes, not just in the US but around the world, is not lost on me. I have to stop thinking about this because whenever I do, it makes me want to call the date off. I mean the meeting—this is not a date, I remind myself one last time before getting out of the car.

The place is busier than I expect for a Sunday afternoon, which is disappointing since the only reason I've decided to meet at this time is I thought it would be slow. I've been here on multiple occasions and I can't remember a time when it was this hectic. People are rushing from every direction, it's almost mayhem. As I glance around the room, I notice an area toward the rear section of the café buzzing with commotion. A group of people are gathered around something. It appears to be a party of some sort, and some patrons are taking pictures with their smartphones. That explains the unusually busier atmosphere.

The more I pay attention, the more it starts to appear odd. If this is a party, then why are some people leaving the crowd, while others stay to take more photos? I walk toward them to find out what all the fuss is about.

Oh. Now I understand. The closer I get, the more obvious it becomes.

"Hey Travis, how long are you going to be in Seattle?" I hear someone yell.

It's Travis being swarmed by a group of fans. "Excuse me," I say as I elbow my way into the crowd, and when Travis sees me, he stands up and moves toward me.

"Let's get out of here. Did you drive?" Travis asks quietly.

As we make our way outside, a new group of fans, along with a growing number of paparazzi, start to flood the entrance of the restaurant, blocking our way. I look to Travis for guidance, figuring he's developed many ways to get himself out of this kind of situation, but when he doesn't do anything and puts his hands up to his face to shield his eyes from the flashing lights of the cameras, I take over.

I grab his hand as I push everyone out of the way, yelling "excuse me," and lead him outside, away from the mess. Thankful that my car is parked just a few feet from the restaurant, I open the door and let Travis in the passenger seat.

The paparazzi are still taking pictures as I get in the car. Both of his hands are covering his face and I can't help but feel bad for him. *Is this what his life is like?* Not wasting any time, I start the car and drive away from the growing mob.

Chapter Eleven

A couple of paparazzi are riding scooters and following closely when I look in my rear-view mirror. And because I know the city like the back of my hand, I drive up and down the alleys, make sharp turns and cross streets at red lights, and this loses them. When there's no sign of them anymore, I finally slow down.

Travis' breathing has grown heavy and he is staring at the dashboard, lost in thought. I give him a couple of minutes to work through whatever he needs to.

"Trav?" I say after waiting, dividing my attention between him and the road. I say his name one more time and when he doesn't answer, I hesitantly place my right hand on his lap to get his attention. Even with his jeans on, I can feel the warmth radiating from him and that sends tremors through my body. I grip the steering wheel tighter to prevent my hand from shaking from the contact.

Still not saying anything and not knowing if I crossed a line, I try to pull my hand back. To my surprise, Travis stops me and places it back where it was, and puts his hand over mine. If I was trembling then, I am in full-on convulsions now. Well, not literally.

It feels like all my nerve endings gather around where my hand meets Travis'. I can feel the roughness of his palm, calloused by all the training, and his pulse that beats from his wrist. Focusing on the road has become more taxing as all my attention is now on Travis and our joined hands. I don't have a lot of guy friends, but I can bet my life that they don't do this.

I take a deep breath that sounds shaky, even for me, and try to focus my attention on the road. Out of the corner of my eye, I can see Travis staring at me. I don't look back because I'm afraid he'll see that I'm enjoying his touch more than I want to admit. I cherish the sensation Travis' touch brings, but when he starts rubbing his thumb back and forth on the back of my hand, I break the connection. We're skating on thin ice, and if I'm not careful I might fall through it. And falling is out of the question. Getting over Travis was the hardest thing I've ever had to do, and I don't know if I can do it all over again.

So, I have to stick with the plan. We can only be friends, nothing more, nothing less.

If Travis is surprised by my abrupt change of demeanor, he doesn't show it. He remains quiet. With both of my hands now on the steering wheel, I continue driving.

I pull over and into a small park overlooking a canyon of trees, a place where we used to hang out when we were kids.

Chapter Twelve
Travis

I hadn't expected him to touch me, but I am so glad he did. The connection that I'd been missing has never been clearer. It's Ash. It's always been Ash, and I am not going to jeopardize my only chance at being part of his life. I had promised that friendship was all I was after. Now, I don't know how long I'm going to be able to keep that promise.

This is not what I had in mind when I left the house this morning. I pictured us catching up on our lost time, eating, enjoying each other's company, and having a great time. Instead, a mob of fans and paparazzi threw a wrench into our day.

"Do you always get that?" Ash asks as he parks his car close to a familiar small nature reserve, covered with evergreen pines and yellow-leafed maple trees. An oasis in one of Seattle's busiest neighborhoods.

There are a number of places like this scattered around the city that are off-limits to private developers in order to protect the wildlife that live there.

"Yeah, but that was actually mild," I finally answer, and he acknowledges with a nod.

The mob that formed around me in the restaurant came out of nowhere, catching me off guard. That wasn't the first time it has happened to me—those types of encounters are almost my norm in New York City and all the other big cities I have been to—but it had never happened in Seattle. I guess winning the US Open shines a brighter spotlight on me. I make a mental note to check online to see what images made it out there and what they are saying. I hope they leave Ash alone.

I'm immediately greeted by the faint sound of rushing water from the bottom of the valley below as soon as I get out of the car. The sound is soft enough that it makes me wonder if what I'm hearing is real, or if it's a phantom sense coming from my memories. I remember that a few yards from where we're standing is a trail that leads to the bottom of the gully, and that a few feet from that is a hidden shortcut that Ash and I used to take when we were younger.

The echoing sounds of jays and red-winged black birds surround the lush ravine. The tranquility of the

Chapter Twelve

scene eases all the tension from minutes ago. I suddenly feel light, and the cool air washes away all the stress and worries of the past few days.

I glance at Ash and notice him watching me silently but intently. And because he's Ash and he knows me like no one else does, he refrains from saying anything, giving me time to think.

I purposely change the topic to something other than what just happened in the restaurant and ask, "Do you think the wooden fortress we built is still down there?"

He shrugs. "I don't know. I haven't been here in years."

Unwilling to change the topic, Ash continues, "I don't know how you do it. Having people follow you everywhere you go, always taking pictures. That's got to get old."

"I'm kind of used to it. I just didn't expect Seattle to be like that."

"It's changed over the years."

"I'm sorry about all that. I didn't mean to ruin your day," I apologize, hoping not to have this day turn out to be a complete bust.

"Who said it was ruined?"

"You sure?" I ask.

"Yes, I'm sure. Do you want to check to see if our fort is still there?" Ash hooks his thumb, pointing in the direction of the canyon below.

"Hell yeah!" I exclaim.

I let Ash lead us down the trail and I'm thankful he doesn't take the shortcut. Walking behind him allows me to study him from my favorite angle. He still looks amazing after all these years. He's wearing some almost-too-tight black jeans that are hugging him in all the right places. I had forgotten about his lean runner's legs, below his perfect ass. I could feel a stirring in my own jeans suddenly. Just friends, Travis, just friends.

"See. Not everything has changed. It looks like our fort weathered the storms." Ash's observation brings my mind back to where it belongs, out of the gutter.

"You never told me why you chose sports medicine," I ask again. I don't know why I'm pushing this so much, but the need to know has been eating me up. I could have asked my mom and dad, or his parents, to find out why, but something tells me that I need to hear it from him. I study his face for signs of aggravation about the question, but when I don't see it, I double down. "Is it because of me?"

Ash, staring at the trees, turns away from me. The movement of his back lets me know he is taking deep breaths, possibly to either tell me to get lost or tell me the reason why. A couple more minutes pass and still he doesn't answer. I take my question back.

"You know what, forget I asked," I say, just as he starts speaking.

Chapter Twelve

"Remember when we went to the ER after your first injury?" Ash says.

"Yeah, how could I forget my first injury?"

"You were so scared, and I felt so helpless about the way that doctor treated us while we were there. It was so awful; it still makes me mad when I think about him."

"I had never seen you that mad, before or after that day," I admit.

"You should have seen me the morning after you left." I don't hear any bitterness or anger in Ash's statement. The way he speaks is very nonchalant and the guilt that is associated with that event six years ago makes me want to express regret once again.

"I'm sorry, Ash. I..."

"Trav, please stop apologizing. You've said you're sorry plenty. If you really want to try this friendship thing, you have to stop saying sorry."

"Sorry. I mean, I'm not sorry," I say.

"You're not? Why?" he asks, but before he can stop himself, he smiles. He actually smiles like my Ash smiles. The smile that makes his blue eyes sparkle. The smile that makes him look younger than twenty-six years old. The smile that makes you smile back like an idiot. The smile that makes me feel like I'm home.

"No, I am not sorry," I joke.

"Good."

"Now, back to our favorite doctor." I make a hand gesture to urge him to keep going, which he does, and I cross my arms over my chest exaggeratedly. That makes him smile more, followed by a dramatic eye roll.

"Right, I made a promise to myself then, that I would do every single thing I could to get into medical school, so I wouldn't feel helpless ever again if you hurt yourself. Seven years later, voila!" he explains and poses as if presenting himself.

I don't know what to say. I suspected that his decision had something to do with me, but hearing him say that is so overwhelming. There are so many things I want to say, but they will not come out and before I can overthink it, I cut the distance between us and hug him tightly. I don't know how he's going to react, but I breathe a big sigh of relief when he hugs me back.

I hug him for all that I'm worth, hoping, just like before, that it conveys all I want to say. Because there are no words to describe what I am feeling about this man.

"Thank you," I say as we pull apart.

"How long are you in town," he asks as soon as we have some space between us.

"Through the holidays. I'm supposed to go to China next month, but I'm thinking of skipping the rest of the season."

Chapter Twelve

"Including the year-end championships in London?" he asks with a look of shock.

"Look at you, are you a big tennis fan now?" I tease.

"I know a thing or two."

"You google me a lot, don't you?"

"Oh please, don't flatter yourself. You're not that famous."

"Hello? Didn't we just get swarmed by paparazzi and a mob of Travis-worshiping fans trying to get a piece of this?" I strike a pose.

"First off, there were two or three paparazzi and maybe a dozen fans. It's not like you're Roger Federer or Serena Williams. I mean, you only have four Grand Slam championships," he taunts.

"Oh, really now! You sure know a lot about my stats for someone who's not impressed by me. Admit it, Ash, you think I'm pretty awesome."

He's staring at me again. I notice him doing that a lot. "I don't think you're awesome. I know you're awesome."

My heart is floating on cloud nine after his last statement and I can't help but feel hopeful. Maybe having Ash back as a friend is exactly what I need to ignite the spark that has been missing in my life these past few years.

"I'm going to the cabin next weekend. Do you wanna go?" I ask.

"What?" Ash acts so surprised that I don't think he heard my question.

"Remember the cabin we used to visit every winter?" I elaborate.

"I know that. But why are you asking me?"

"I figure it would be fun. You know, catch up."

"I don't think that's a good idea, Trav. Plus, I'm on call that weekend."

"I get it. I just thought I'd ask." I try my best not to sound defeated.

"Trav, I do want to be friends. I just don't think it's a good idea," he explains.

Even though I expected him to say no, the rejection still stings. He's quiet for a while and, just like that, the progress I thought we had made with our friendship is gone and the awkwardness returns and tension lingers.

The fragility of our relationship is something I had never expected. We used to be able to read each other's minds and finish each other's statements. Now, one question can turn us from friends to strangers in the blink of an eye. And I only have myself to blame.

Chapter Thirteen
Ashton

Wanna go with me? I'm still thinking about Travis' question when an overhead page broadcasts an urgent call, instructing me and the other residents to report to the emergency room.

After receiving the briefings of the call, Katie and I are both on our cellphones with operating room staff as we rush downstairs with our attendings. Today is the first day of our trauma rotation and we've been on a mission since we learned about a serious multi-car crash on Interstate Five heading into Seattle.

We're making calls to reserve the OR now and it will save a lot of time once the patients arrive. Time under these circumstances is vital.

The trauma rotation is required to successfully complete our sports medicine residency, and it's the one that I'm least looking forward to. I recite everything that I learned about orthopedic trauma to myself to prepare for what's to come through the hospital doors.

We pick up our pace when the sound of sirens gets louder, and since hallways are empty at this wee hour of the night, we run.

We meet three ambulances at the entrance to the hospital. The scene that follows can only be described as complete chaos—there are sirens wailing, lights flashing, and screams coming from inside the ambulance cabs.

One by one, the back doors of the ambulances open and the EMTs remove each gurney that holds patients with different levels of trauma. The chief resident calls our names and pairs us with each attending. Dr. Kirkland, my attending, is assigned to the patient in the most critical condition. This victim will require lifesaving surgery before we can operate on any broken bones.

I start pushing the gurney with the assistance of another intern, who is guiding in front and letting everyone know to get out of the way. The EMT starts flipping through his chart notes as he gives us the updated status of our patient, who is unresponsive and intubated. The readout on the small device attached to the patient's right index finger is getting low, which is never a good sign because it means the patient's oxygen level is declining fast.

Chapter Thirteen

"Do we have an ID?" I ask the EMT.

"His name is Andrew Howard. Thirty-eight years old, according to his driver's license." He continues to walk with us to answer our questions that pertain to our patient, but stops when we reach the elevator leading us to the operating room. I direct him to the intake desk so he can give them any information that will assist staff with locating his family.

A group of nurses and technologists take over the patient as they begin to prep him for what may be multiple surgeries. Two thoracic surgeons start scrubbing their hands all the way up to their elbows as they give Dr. Kirkland and I the plan for the first surgery.

My focus shifts to the patient now lying on the operating table. The glass window separates the sterile operating room from the outside, where the sinks are located. I turn to Dr. Kirkland.

"Is he going to be okay?" I ask.

"I don't know," he says. "He's bleeding from the inside and we'll have to wait until that surgery is completed before we can operate on his crushed leg. That has to happen immediately if we're to have a chance of saving his leg."

"So, what do we do?"

"We wait."

The surgery to repair the patient's ruptured pulmonary artery, a major blood vessel in the lungs and lower intestine, took almost four hours, and after they closed his torso, we began prepping his legs, starting with the worst one, his right leg.

The extent of his right femur fracture is worse than it looked from the X-ray taken prior to the surgery. It will take multiple plates and screws to repair the broken bones, and the rehab that will come after that will be so comprehensive it'll take months before he will be able to walk on his own.

"What's going on up there?" Dr. Kirkland asks the anesthesiologist, as an alarm coming from one of the monitors hooked to the patient starts beeping. His laser focus on the procedure is so intense that he doesn't even look up to see what the alarm is for.

"Patient's pulse and blood pressure is dropping," the anesthesiologist says as she gets up from her chair to check. The alarm keeps going and when Dr. Kirkland stops what he's doing, I begin to worry.

"What can I do, Dr. Kirkland?" I ask while holding the retractor, but before he can answer, the monitor flat lines and that's when he orders me to perform CPR.

"What? But—"

"Dr. Kennedy, now!"

With trembling hands, I start putting pressure on the patient's chest, the same chest that was open just minutes ago. I keep applying pressure but when

Chapter Thirteen

there are still no signs of life after four attempts, Dr. Kirkland takes over. One of the OR nurses rushes a defibrillator cart to us, and Dr. Kirkland rubs a pair of palm-size paddles together, shouts "clear!" and charges the patient's chest with the paddles. The anesthesiologist administers a dose of epinephrine after his order, and Dr. Kirkland repeats the procedure three more times, as I watch the monitor for any sign of movement.

After multiple unsuccessful attempts to revive our patient, the room turns quiet. One of the worst moments of my life comes when Dr. Kirkland calls the patient's time of death. The realization that for the very first time I have lost a patient hits me like a freight train. One plug after another is unhooked from the monitors and the room empties. I stay where I am, my gaze still on the now-silent machines.

Dr. Kirkland comes around and stands next to me. "Ash, it's not your fault. It's no one's fault. The complications from all the injuries he sustained caused his cardiac arrest. We did everything we could to save him," he places his hand on my shoulder.

"He was only thirty-eight years old," I say, and a long pause follows.

"Shall I speak with the family alone?" he offers.

"No, I'll do it with you."

The waiting area outside the OR is full of people. A young woman pacing back and forth notices our approach and hurries toward us, bumping into several people on her way. Her swollen eyes ringed with running mascara lead me to believe she must be the wife.

"My name is Jill Howard. My husband is Andrew. They told me that Andrew is having surgery," she says, her voice rising, getting more hysterical with every question. "Are you his doctors? Is he going to be okay?"

"Mrs. Howard, my name is Dr. Kennedy, and this is my attending, Dr. Kirkland. There were some complications during the surgery, and I'm so sorry to—"

"No! No! No!" she screams. "Please tell me he's still alive. Tell me he's going to be okay. Please. Please!"

"I am so sorry. We tried everything we could to save him, but his body suffered multiple traumas from the accident, and they caused too many complications. I am terribly sorry." The agony on her face the moment she hears my words is awful. Her sorrow is more than I can bear and in that moment all I want to do is run. But I do my best to remain strong as I lead Mrs. Howard to an available room so we can speak in private.

How do you ask a grief-stricken spouse if they are willing to give the gift of life?

Chapter Fourteen
Travis

I'm awakened by the buzzing sound of my alarm clock that I set the night before, and I reach out to the nightstand and hit snooze for another five minutes. My hope of getting a few more minutes of sleep is disrupted when the second alarm clock starts beeping, the one that I also set the night before anticipating that the first alarm would not be enough to wake my sorry ass. And since this alarm is sitting on top of the dresser across the room, I have to get up, which had been my intention when I set it up last night. I sometimes hate it when things happen the way you intend them to.

I put on my fleece robe that's laying on the chair next to my nightstand, and walk like a zombie to turn off the alarm. I go straight to the bathroom to do my usual morning routine and when I'm somewhat awake,

I head out of my room and downstairs to the kitchen to make a cup of coffee.

However, the unexpected smell of a fresh brew greets me as I reach the kitchen. I see my dad sitting on one of the bar stools while reading the paper, a cup of coffee in his other hand.

"Good morning, son," he greets me, and I must be sporting a scowl on my face because he follows with, "Still not a morning person, I see."

"Dad, it's five o'clock in the morning. Do you always get up this early?" I ask as I manage to make it to the coffee pot without banging my knees on anything.

"No, I just wanted to make sure I said goodbye before you head out to the cabin."

"You didn't have to do that, Dad," I say, before the first sip of coffee hits my mouth.

"I know. But I wanted to tell you that the weather forecast said there will be snow up there."

"This early? It's only late September."

"I know. But the foothills of Mt. Rainer are very unpredictable, and they're having an unseasonably cold fall. With added moisture, it's a recipe for an early snowstorm."

"Good to know, thanks Dad. I'll throw a couple of my winter coats in the car," I say, sounding more myself now that I've consumed a half-cup of coffee.

"Drive the truck. It's better for those conditions. I

Chapter Fourteen

already put the tire chains in the back just in case you need them."

"Okay, Dad. Thanks. You're the best!" I give him a hug to show my appreciation. Not just for today, but for always making sure that I'm okay.

"Of course, son. What time are you heading out?"

"In an hour. I just have to get ready. I'm packed and I'll get the groceries on my way."

"It's too bad Ash can't come with you. That kid needs a break. It seems like all he does is study and work. It would've been good for him to get away."

"I know, Dad. Maybe next time."

I also wished that he was going, but as much as it disappoints me, I understood why he chose not to. This was probably for the best, because what I needed to do was to clear my head and not worry about anything for a couple of days. No tennis, no fans, no paparazzi, no Ash.

It's still dark out when I leave my parents' house. The roads are quiet as most people are sleeping in for the weekend. It doesn't take me long to reach the freeway, where I head south out of the city. I turn the radio to a local rock station to keep me entertained for the next three hours.

An hour into my drive, my phone rings and Aaliyah's name appears on the screen.

"Aaliyah, how's New York?" I ask, talking to her through the truck's Bluetooth.

"Boring as shit without you. Why are you up this early? I was hoping to get your voicemail."

"I'm driving out of town."

"Then why did you answer if you're driving? Travis, you know how I feel about texting and driving. I'll call you back."

"Haven't you heard of hands-free, girl?"

"Hands-free? I love sex talk as much as the next gal, but it's too early for that."

"Ewww. I meant Bluetooth, you perve."

"Just kidding. But since I have you on the phone, I just wanted to let you know that Evan St. John has been looking for you. He wants me to set up a meeting, but I told him that you're out of town and might not be back until next month."

Evan has been my mentor since before I turned pro, and he's been instrumental in my career. He's helped me with my game and some personal stuff that happened in the past. "He said that you haven't been answering his repeated calls," she continues.

"I know. I feel bad. The past couple of weeks have been so crazy, that's why I'm going away for the weekend. To relax. Me, myself, and I."

"Is everything okay? Is this getting too much?"

"No, of course not. I didn't mean to worry you. I'll be fine. I just need a break."

"You know I'm here for you. Whatever you need. Just call."

Chapter Fourteen

"I know. But hey, listen, it's starting to snow, and I want to focus on driving. I'll call you when I get back since there won't be any reception where I'm going."

"Take care of yourself, Travis, and don't hesitate to call if you need anything."

"Will do. Bye."

The temperature is steadily declining as I reach Crystal Mountain, where the cabin is located. I stop by the grocery store to buy the things I'll need for the next few days, and when I get out of the store the snow is falling heavier. I hurry to the car so I can get to the cabin before it gets worse.

It doesn't take me long to find our family cabin in the middle of the woods, just off the only road to Crystal Mountain. The snow that blankets the cabin and the entire surroundings muffles the sounds of the forest, animals and humans alike. The eerie silence reminds me of how isolated I am from everywhere and everyone.

***

Nine years ago

Ash and I put on our snowshoes after breakfast to explore the woods outside my parents' cabin, where we were spending the rest of the midwinter break. I hadn't been sure if his mom would let him spend an entire week away from home, but because my parents and his were good friends, they were able to assure them they would take good care of him and that he was safe with us.

"Mom, Dad, we're heading out," I told my parents once we were laced.

"Don't go too far. I heard another snowstorm is coming," Mom warned us.

"We won't. We'll be back in a couple of hours," Ash said.

The top frozen layer of snow crunched as we made our way down the trail that led to the patch of woods that separated the cabin and the small frozen pond. A few feet from where we were walking, a small shrub was shaking and the snow covering its leaves started to fall.

"Ash," I whispered to get his attention. I slowly brought my index finger to my lips to make sure he stayed quiet and I used the same finger to point in the direction of the shaking plant.

"What is it?" he whispered back as he walked toward me.

"Cougar," I teased, and his eyes widened.

"What? Let's get out of here." He started heading in the opposite direction.

"I'm kidding. It's probably just a snow bunny. And even if it is a big cat, you're not supposed to turn your back on one."

Chapter Fourteen

"I know that," he said, but I didn't believe him.

"Let's keep going." I urged him on.

We moved forward, and when we got closer to the shrub, a rabbit with white fur jumped out of the bush and caught Ash off guard. He jumped back so quickly that his abrupt move, along with the awkward snowshoes I had on, messed with my balance. I fell back and he landed on top of me.

We started laughing and when he turned around to face me, our eyes met. He was breathing heavily and the fog between our faces became thick. His eyes moved to my lips and he swallowed hard. His eyes came back to mine and there was a look in them that I had never seen before. I moved my head closer to judge his reaction, and when his look intensified, I licked my lips in anticipation. I don't remember who made the first move, but before I knew it, his soft lips were on mine.

Neither of us had kissed someone before, let alone another guy. Ash and I had been best friends for almost a decade and we'd never done anything like this. I've known since Ash was fifteen, when he came out to me, that he was gay, but he didn't know that I was too. Actually, no one knew, and I planned to keep it that way.

"I'm so sorry, Trav. I didn't mean to do that," he said as he broke away. He looked so flustered and I debated if now would be the time to tell him my truth. He stood up and removed his snowshoes in a hurry. He ran back to the cabin, following our previous tracks, as fast as he could to get away from me.

I lay there for a second while I processed what had just happened. It finally clicked. That kiss proved to me what I had been feeling toward Ash. I loved him. And not just because we were best friends. I *loved* him. I was in love with my best friend. I was in love with Ash.

A few more minutes passed, and I got up and dusted the remaining snow from my coat and headed back to the cabin.

"Where's Ash?" I asked my mom while I untied my shoes.

"He's in your room. Is everything okay? He came in in a hurry and when we asked him where you were, he didn't answer."

"Yeah, everything's okay. I'll go check on him."

My nerves were out of control when I made my way to the bedroom I shared with Ash. I didn't bother knocking and when I got inside, he was standing by the window looking toward the door, as if he had been waiting for me. A look of worry was painted all over his face as he bit his lower lip, a telltale sign that he was in distress. I reached behind myself, subtly locked the door, and walked toward him.

Chapter Fourteen

"I'm so sorry, Trav. I didn't know what I was doing. I just got carried away..." I reached out and held his face and kissed him to stop him from saying anything else. I noticed that his eyes grew wide from the shock.

"Don't be sorry," I said after we took a break from kissing to catch our breaths.

"Wait, are you...are you gay?" he asked.

Instead of answering, I just nodded my head—*yes*. His eyes danced with joy and I kissed him again.

"Is it okay if we keep it a secret for now," I asked.

"Of course."

The rest of that weekend with Ash in a shared bed was the fondest memory I had to date.

Chapter Fifteen
Ashton

I'm sitting in the darkest corner of the residents' locker room with my back against the wall when the door opens. I look up to see Katie walking toward me with a bottle of water in one hand and a banana in the other. It's been a couple of hours since my conversation with Mrs. Howard, and Katie's presence means that she's heard about what happened to my patient in the operating room.

I pull my knees closer to my chest when she's standing in front of me.

"You should have seen his wife, Katie. The pain. The agony. It was...too much." Just when I think I have no more tears left to cry, more of them fall, and I don't even bother hiding them. "He was only thirty-eight years old."

Chapter Fifteen

Katie sits beside me and wraps her arm around my shoulder. She doesn't say anything. She just lets us sit in silence.

"It's so unfair. Imagine the love of your life leaving one morning, not knowing that it will be the last time you see them. I wish I could have done something more."

"Ash, sweetie. It's not your fault. His body gave up and you tried everything you could. This is not on you," she affirms, sincerity obvious in her voice.

My chest feels tight from the heavy emotions and my breathing has become more labored as a result of my continuous sobbing. I'm not sure what happens, but the next thing I know Katie is sitting in front of me with both of her hands on my shoulders.

"Ash, try to breathe slower and deeper for me, okay." I nod. "Let's do it together, okay."

I'm on the verge of hyperventilating.

"One," she instructs and we inhale.

"Two." We exhale.

"Three." And so on and so on...

I start to feel better at the count of five, and as I do, my pager starts beeping. Before I can pull it out of the case on my waistband, Katie grabs it and reads the message. She walks to the nearest phone on the wall and dials the number, presumably to call the page sender.

"No, this isn't Dr. Kennedy. This is Dr. Harrison," she introduces herself and a long pause follows. "You can assign those patients to me and I'll talk to the attendings." Another pause follows and Katie looks back at me. "That sounds like a plan. Thank you."

"You didn't have to do that. I'll be fine. I just needed a minute," I say after she ends the call.

"No, you are not fine. Look at you. Why don't you head home and take the next few days off? I'll take care of your patients and I'll put myself on call for the weekend."

"I'll be fine, I promise," I protest.

"This is non-negotiable, Ash. I am dead serious. It's okay to accept help once in a while. I know you think that you have to do everything on your own, but trust me when I say you are not fine." The look on her face says it all. I'm not going to win this argument with her. All I manage to do is nod in agreement, too spent to talk, let alone argue.

"And please eat something," she orders, grabbing the water and banana from the bench and handing them to me.

"Thank you. You're a good friend," I say.

She gives me a kiss on the cheek. "Take care of yourself, okay. And call if you need anything."

After a quick shower, I change into my street clothes, leave the hospital, and get into my car to drive home.

Chapter Fifteen

I am physically and emotionally exhausted, and I can't get the image of Mrs. Howard out of my head. The anguish on her face knowing that she will never see her husband again, kiss him again, tell him how much she loves him again, is occupying my every thought. If she could have another minute with her husband, what would she do? What would she say to him?

I keep driving but my hands seem to have minds of their own. I need to take the next exit, but my heart wants something else, and so I pass it by. I know what it wants, and I keep going with that destination in mind.

Chapter Sixteen
Travis

The inside of the cabin is exactly how I remember it. This is the place where our family used to go during midwinter breaks in February, but after Cole got married and I went to college, it rarely gets used. In fact, the smell of stale air that greets me when I open the door and the dust covering the furniture is a sign that no one has used this place in a long while. I leave the door open to clear the musty smell, but when the wind blows snow inside, I shut it.

I take off my shoes to prevent tracking in snow and dirt, and since the temperature inside the cabin is as cold as it is outside, I keep my coat on. I go straight to the kitchen to drop off the groceries I bought earlier and before doing anything else, I decide to start the fire to warm the cabin.

Chapter Sixteen

I grab four medium-sized logs from the stack next to the fireplace made out of river rocks. I brush spiderwebs off the logs before laying them crisscrossed on the metal grate, and then light the fire using some old matches.

I keep busy for the next few hours putting food away and cleaning up to make the cabin comfortable for the weekend. I start to sweat as the cabin warms up, so I take my coat off and hang it on one of the hooks beside the door. I've only been here for a couple of hours and the isolation that I thought would help me unwind is starting to make me uneasy. And without access to the internet, I feel disconnected.

The thing about voluntary isolation is, you have to love yourself. Truthfully, I don't even like myself, let alone love myself. All the lying and hiding is taking its toll on me and makes me question if I'm making the right decision. Sometimes, it feels like the greater my achievements are, the lonelier I become.

I make my way to the bedroom to change into more comfortable clothes, and I pass a series of framed black-and-white pictures from all the vacations we'd taken as a family. My heart stops when my eyes land on the photo of me and Ash. The image was taken when we were seventeen years old, which was the same year we kissed for the first time and when I revealed the real me. I knew that I loved him then, but I was too much of a coward to admit it. Ash always thought of me as the stronger of the two of us, but he was the bravest. I wonder what he thinks of me now. I walk away to stop the profound sense of loneliness that wants to envelop me. Something tells me that it already did.

My bare feet feel incredible soaking up the heat from the fire. The open floor plan of the cabin allows the place to warm up quickly, so I strip down to my boxers and an old UCLA t-shirt that has seen better days. I'm sitting on the chair by the fire when the distinct crunching sound of tires rolling across gravel catches my attention. Is my mind playing tricks on me? It's probably just the wind, or perhaps the three generous glasses of wine I've consumed since I settled in for the night.

It's only a matter of time before the weather turns into a full-blown storm. The snow has been falling steadily for hours, and layers upon layers of snow cover the ground since the last time I checked when I'd topped off my glass of wine. If I had planned better, I would have brought the bottle back with me to the fire. Well, at least, I can do a sobriety check each time I walk to the counter for another refill. It's early, I haven't even gotten through a bottle. Yet.

I reach for my final sip before my next sobriety-test trip to the kitchen and stand up just as there is a faint knock on the door. Who the hell could that be? The

Chapter Sixteen

cabin is secluded, in the middle of nowhere, and I'm not expecting anyone tonight—or ever.

I look down at my boxers and bare legs to decide if my state of undress is decent enough to open the door. Another knock comes from the door, this one louder.

"Who is it?" I ask, as I look around for something I can use as a weapon and settle for a fireplace poker. I grab the metal rod and slowly walk toward the door. "How can I help you?" I ask, trying to hide my shaking voice. When still there's no answer, I cautiously open the door while gripping my makeshift weapon, ready to strike if necessary. I've seen those cabin-in-the-woods slasher flicks. I'm not dying today.

Shock wouldn't even begin to describe my reaction when I find out who my unexpected guest is. I shake my head to make sure I'm not hallucinating or dreaming.

"Ash? What are you—?" I'm about to ask him what he's doing here when his eyes fill with tears and he rushes toward me. His hug is so strong, it's borderline painful. But I don't care. I usher him inside and use my foot to slam the door shut to prevent the freezing air from following us in.

His face is cold and his whole body is shivering. His hold on me tightens as I try to free myself from his embrace to pull the wool blanket off the leather chair.

"It's okay, Ash, I'm not going anywhere," I say. I extend my arm, still holding him, and yank the blanket from the chair. I drape it over his shoulders and walk him to the fire to get him warm.

I look at him as his face gives way to a full cascade of emotions, and he drops his chin to his chest in defeat.

"Ash, what's wrong? Are you okay? Are you hurt? Did someone hurt you?" I ask. The overwhelming need to shield him from anything that could hurt him kicks into gear and I'm ready to fight whoever is responsible for his pain.

He shakes his head *no* and even with the blanket covering him, he's still trembling. I hug him tight as I rub my hands all over his back, hoping the friction will help warm up his freezing body. I don't know how long we're in that position, but when his shaking finally stops, he loosens his hold on me and raises his head to meet my gaze.

I feel his breath on my lips and the unmistakable look of desire in his eyes burns a hundred times hotter than the fire that is keeping us warm.

Ashton leans forward, giving me a gentle push. And then another, then another, without taking his eyes off mine. He places his hands on my shoulders and slowly moves me backward.

Chapter Sixteen

I scan his face. "What are you doing?" I ask, but he doesn't answer. He continues to advance on me; step by step, I'm being maneuvered back to the old leather chair I had been sitting on just minutes ago.

"Sit," he demands.

"What?" I nervously look around to see if I've been pushed close enough to sit down. I reach behind me to secure a hand on the thick leather arm of the chair. Ash doesn't take his eyes off mine as he stands staring down at me. He pulls his arms through his parka and tosses it behind him onto the floor. The remaining snowflakes that haven't melted float in the air, back-lit by the fire that leads them to their slow death.

Ash kneels in front me slowly while daring me to take my eyes off him. He reaches forward and lays his hands on my knees.

"Do you want me to stop?" he asks. Speechless, the most I can do is move my head left and right. *No.*

In one swift move, he spreads my knees apart. I gasp with the anticipation of what's to come and my body tightens.

"Relax, Trav," he orders, as his hands begin a slow march up the inside of each exposed leg. The pressure increases as he heads up an inch at a time. I feel my erection stir as he approaches the final section of bare skin, reaching the bottom edge of my boxers.

Ash corks a seductive smile, then shifts his eyes down to my swelling underwear. One hand remains steady on my thigh, while the other slides into the small opening in the boxers, where he spreads two fingers wide to reveal my now solid cock. He pauses for a second to gauge my reaction, to make sure I'm in this.

"Please. Don't stop," I beg, not caring if I sound needy.

That seems to be all he needs to hear as he resumes his slow torment. The same fingers that have exposed my cock now relieve it from its confinement and he holds me in his hand. He slides his thumb over the head of my throbbing cock that's glistening with pre-cum, discovering the first signs of what's to come. He places the other hand on my abs to support himself as he leans forward. I watch as my thick swollen dick slides into his mouth.

"Fuck!"

Ash manages to slide the length of my cock into his mouth in one sweet gulp. I haven't had my dick in a mouth since the last time we'd been together this way. I forgot how amazing he feels and how talented he is. I push my hips forward as he slides his free hand into the bottom of my boxers and hunts for my sack.

"Oh, baby," I groan.

I reach out to participate and get a rough slap on my hand. He pushes my stomach hard and forces me back into the chair.

Wanting more and more of me in him, I lift my hips off the chair and force myself deeper. He gags and as his eyes become glossy from both tears and lust, he pauses for a second. I haven't been with anyone since Ash and I don't know if he's been with anyone since me. The thought of Ash with someone else is something that I don't want to dwell on at this particular moment. Because right now, he's with me and it's my dick in his mouth. And that is all that matters.

He's slobbering up and down my length and squeezing my nuts as his muffled noises get louder with each pump of my hips.

I haven't shot a load with a partner in way too many years, so I know I won't be holding out much longer.

"Ash, I'm getting..." I pant. "I'm getting close. Don't stop." Another pant.

I feel the orgasm building and I know I'll be blasting my load out at any second.

"Oh, fuck, baby, I'm coming." My hips spring forward as I bury my seed deep in his mouth. The ecstasy.

"That felt amazing, Ash. Holy shit!"

I remain seated as he walks four feet away to the couch. He keeps his back to me as he uses his feet to pull his shoes off one by one. He grabs the bottom edge of his sweatshirt, pulls it over his head and tosses it on the floor.

His back is smooth and lean. He still has that V shape that tapers down to his slim waist. I watch as his hands move to his belt buckle to undo it. The sound of the zipper going down follows and I know the jeans are next. His strip tease is doing all sorts of things to me and my cock starts to revive.

As I continue to watch in anticipation, he moves his fingers inside of his jeans along the waist band. He slowly pushes his jeans down off his hips. Motherfucker! He's going commando.

Ash leans down to grab an ankle as he slides his feet out of each pant leg. His smooth ass, firm from running, is just the right size, each cheek a handful and curved to perfection.

"Don't move," I demand of him. "Stay right where you are."

I watch as he stands up with his back to me. He doesn't move a muscle. I sit there staring at his exposed backside. Fuck, he is so goddamn gorgeous.

It's been way too long since I've seen this particular ass. I stand up and step out of my boxers, pull my t-shirt off, and walk a few feet behind him. He still doesn't move. Not even an inch. I decide to take my sweet time as I admire the view. I miss that body, that ass. It's going to be a great return home.

I take three steps forward but don't touch him. He quivers as he feels my breath inches from the back of his neck. I wait as I see him tremble at the idea of what's to come.

Reaching out with one hand, I cup a butt cheek in my palm, gently applying pressure to it. Another step forward and the other hand cups his other cheek.

Chapter Sixteen

I breathe on his neck and lean into him as I apply more pressure to his ass, lifting it up as I lean harder on him. I open my mouth and kiss the back of his neck. He remains still and has his arms at his side. Pulling one of his arms backward, I guide it to my raging hard-on. "See what you still do to me, Kennedy?" I moan. "How could you ever think I could let you go? Feel that cock? You may regret draining the first load. I think you remember what I can do the second time around, don't you?"

I drop to my knees and push him forward onto the couch. Putting my hands on the inside of his knees, I push them apart.

"Do you remember the first time I did this to you?" He shivers slightly.

I stick a finger in my mouth and wet it generously. I place my hand at the top of his ass crack and begin a slow journey down the crease to his welcoming hole. Ash shudders as I slide my fingertip to his entrance. I push my other hand between his legs and hold his nuts in my hand. His cock is at full attention. I had played with his thick and long cock many times. It may have been an exceptionally long time since, but a man knows his lover's body when he returns to it.

I tap his ass to get him to lift his knees. He moves his knees up and onto the couch and grabs the back of it with his hands. I spread his legs apart, but then stop what I'm doing. He jerks his head around to look at me, confused with the sudden halt.

"I don't have any condoms," I say, disappointed.

"I haven't been with anybody since you and I just got tested when I had my physical last month," he says.

"I haven't been with anyone either," I admit. I want to ask him why he hasn't been with anyone since me, but I know right now is not the time.

"Then let's do it like we've always done."

"Are you sure?" I ask and he nods. "Don't move, I'll be right back."

I jog down the hall to the bedroom where my duffel bag is stored, to grab a small bottle of lube I keep for jacking off, and rush back to a waiting Ash.

My excitement grows when I return, if that's even possible, and I remove the cap from the lube bottle and smear a small amount to his waiting hole. After applying the lube to him, I spread it up and down my shaft. I position the head of my dick against his opening. I apply a little more pressure as he willingly allows me inside. After a few moments go by, he urges me to keep going and it doesn't take long before I'm plunging into him deeper with every thrust. The primal sounds coming from Ash let me know he's loving it as much as I am. I grab his hips and pump harder in response to his pleasure.

Chapter Sixteen

I turn him over to his back so I can see his beautiful face. I lift his ankles over my shoulders and take aim at his hole, plunging back in deep. His eyes roll back and he throws his hands over his head, exposing all of himself to me.

"Oh my god, Trav," he calls out. The sound of my name on his lips while he's in ecstasy is all I need to drive me over the edge.

I spit in my hand and reach down to grab his erection. I stroke it slowly at first and then start applying pressure and speed in rhythm with my thrusts, plowing into his ass harder each time.

"Keep going. Don't stop, I'm gonna come, Trav!" I feel my body flexing as it builds the next explosion to come. I keep my eyes trained on Ash as he moans. He yells my name one last time as jets of cum fly up to his stomach. My orgasm follows and I fill his ass with my cum. We are both totally and completely spent. It's then that I collapse onto him and our mouths meet for the first time.

Chapter Seventeen
Ashton

I've had enough disappointments to last someone two lifetimes and it took losing a patient to realize how stuck I've become. I've been so angry these past six years that I built a wall so tall I became its prisoner. A prison where it was just me and the constant voices in my head that keep telling me I'm not good enough. That I will never be good enough.

If Mrs. Howard could have another minute with her husband, what would she do? What would she say to him? The question I asked Katie about the grieving widow kept playing in my head long after she was gone. Unlike her, I still have a chance to do what I want to do and say what I want to say. That's how I ended up here—with Travis.

After we make love in the living room, we continue exploring each other, rediscovering every curve, every

Chapter Seventeen

muscle, and every freckle of our bodies. We make our way to his bedroom, where we share another mind-blowing connection that leads to the best orgasm ever.

Sweaty and covered with our own releases, Travis invites me to shower with him. Because I don't want this moment to end, I let him pull me off his bed and lead me to the bathroom.

Travis turns on the shower and the bathroom quickly fogs up with steam. As we step under the water, its pressure and warmth release all the anxiety I've been carrying since I left the hospital.

Travis reaches across me to grab the bar of soap, while I take the shampoo and put a small amount on my hand. I turn around to face him and I start lathering his hair as he soaps my chest. He asks me to turn around so my back is facing him, and he continues his attention to my neck, down to my back, and then the curve of my ass, where he spends an extra amount of time.

We switch positions, so he shampoos my hair as I rub soap all over his body, paying special attention to his chest, my favorite part of him. We take turns rinsing each other off and, without saying any words, we're able to convey all the things we want to say to each other with our touches and our kisses. Just like when we were together six years before.

I reach out to turn the shower off and Travis plants a kiss on me once again.

We're laying on the bed facing each other while our legs are tangled under the flannel sheet. Our hands ghost over every exposed part of our bodies as we listen to the swooshing sound of snow and wind outside, and the endless tapping of a small tree branch on one of the cabin windows. Travis combs a rogue cluster of hair that is partially covering my eyes. He smiles as his attempt only makes more of my hair fall. After trying several times, the unruly hair behaves and stays put.

"There," he says, and kisses my forehead. The back of his hand slides down my face, outlining my cheekbone and jawline. I don't dare move or speak, fearing that I might do or say something that will break the spell we're under.

We continue the exploration of our bodies while our gazes stay connected. There's a sparkle in Travis' eyes that I haven't seen since we reunited. He seems happy.

The voices in my head return, telling me to run and that I'm making a huge mistake by being here, but I drown them out with the touches from Travis' hand and the kisses of his lips.

"I lost a patient today," I murmur, and Travis sits up and looks at me. His mouth opens wide.

"What? Ash, I am so sorry."

I prop myself up on my elbow so I can face him. He grabs my hand and places it on his lips and kisses it. There's nothing sexual about the kiss; its tenderness is a reminder that he's here for me.

Chapter Seventeen

One by one, I recall every moment with him, and as I do, the pressure in my chest decreases little by little, until the stabbing pain begins to subside. He uses his other hand to wipe away the tears that are falling from my eyes.

"We tried our best, but his body just gave up."

"That must have been awful," he says. All I do is nod.

Understanding that I can't give him any more details about the incident because of patient-doctor confidentiality, we lay back on the bed. I move my head to his chest, where I can hear his steady heartbeat. He's absently running his fingers through my hair and I feel him plant a soft kiss on the top of my head. I run my hands over his chest, tracing every line of his muscles.

"That feels good," he whispers in my ear.

I continue with my caresses, content just to lay with him, willing the time to stop turning and to stay in this moment forever.

I ask him about New York and tennis, while he asks me to tell him about medical school and my residency. The manner of our conversation flows like we haven't spent any time apart. We also talk about his agent-friend, Aaliyah, and I tell him about Katie.

"Katie sounds like fun. I would love to meet her."

"You would? Really?" I ask as I look up at him to see if he's serious. His statement surprises me, and I'm not entirely sure why.

"Yeah, why does that shock you?" he says, grabbing my hand that rests on his abs and kissing it.

"I just didn't think you'd want to meet any of my friends."

"What makes you think that?" he asks.

"Actually, I don't know what made me think that, or why I overthink everything, for that matter," I admit.

"Can I ask you something?" Travis asks after several minutes have passed.

"Sure."

"What's up with you and your mom?"

"What do you mean?" I ask, even though I know exactly what he means.

"I can't put my finger on it."

"Yeah, you can, and you just did," I tease, which is followed by a burst of laughter from Travis.

When he finally recovers, he continues. "I'm serious, you goofball."

I debate whether to tell him the reasons why, afraid that he'll never understand why I reacted the way I did. Because honestly, I'm starting to question it myself.

In the end, I decide to tell him the truth. "Do you want the long story or the cliff notes?"

"Whatever version you're comfortable with."

I take a breath. "Do you remember the night I called you to tell you that I didn't get into Stanford?"

"Of course," he says.

Chapter Seventeen

"Well, I lied, and that was the breaking point. I hadn't received anything from Stanford that week, but I wasn't worried, you know. It was still early, but when my mom found out, she called her friend at the admissions department and used her connections to get me in before knowing whether I had been accepted or not. I was so mad at her, Trav. She's always doing that. She's always using her connections or power to get what she wants. I've worked so hard. I wanted to prove something to myself, that I'm capable on my own. And making that call before we knew anything was so inappropriate." I tell Travis the whole story and he listens intently. He doesn't say anything or offer an opinion, and for that I'm thankful.

Hearing everything spoken out loud makes it sound extremely petty. Sure, what my mother did was wrong, but does it warrant losing her relationship with me? Was I too harsh?

"Have you talked to her?" he finally asks.

"Talk to her about what?"

"About how you feel. Sometimes people make decisions that they think are best for the one they love."

"I don't know. Sometimes I feel like I make mountains out of molehills."

"No, you don't, you should never question how you feel. I'm just saying, maybe hearing what she has to say could change how you feel. Do you understand that?" he reasons.

"Maybe. It's getting late and I'm beat. Mind if we go to bed?"

"We are in bed," he jokes, and I roll my eyes at him.

Travis gives me another kiss and I roll to my side as he wraps his arms around me. I lie there for a while thinking about what he said. Maybe it's time to finally confront my feelings with my mom. Maybe.

"Stop thinking about it. It was just a suggestion," Travis says, as if reading my mind.

"Goodnight, Travis," I reply, and he chuckles.

"Goodnight, Ashton."

Chapter Eighteen
Travis

Waking up from the best sleep I've had in a long time, I reach over to feel Ash on my bed to make sure that last night wasn't a dream. My hand lands on his warm back, and his heavy breathing lets me know he is still asleep.

I carefully get out of bed to avoid waking him up. I don't know anything about his schedule, but if everything I've heard about life as a surgical resident is true, Ash needs as much sleep as he can get.

I walk toward the closet where I'd put my duffel bag. Since I'm only planning on staying for the weekend, I don't bother putting my clothes in the dresser. I put on a fresh pair of boxers and glance one more time at the beautiful man sleeping on my bed before making my way out of the room.

Embers are all that remain from last night's fire.

I start to shiver the moment my feet meet the chilly floor. I should've remembered a second portable heater for the cabin's main room, then perhaps it wouldn't be so damn cold out here. My breaths become visible as I tiptoe to the fireplace. To stay warm as I get the fire going, I pull on the wool blanket that is loosely draped over the chair and slide into my shoes. I feed the fire with a few more logs than I did yesterday, hoping it will warm the cabin faster.

Once satisfied by the blaze, I make my way to the kitchen and start the coffee.

I head back to the fire and add another log for good measure, upon remembering that Ash has never been a fan of the cold. I pull the drapes open in the living room to let natural light in, and I put a hand over my face as my eyes adjust to the brightness from the combination of sun and snow.

The absence of clouds in the blue sky is a contrast to what it was the day before. The snowstorm has stopped and all that's left are small flurries of snowflakes floating in the air from the trees around us. The graveled driveway is no longer visible, and both of our cars are covered by snow and some debris from branches that were unable to carry the weight of the snow they had collected.

The state of chaos brought by the storm is hyperbole for what I'm feeling inside. Every fiber in my body screams *run*, but just like the trees that managed to

Chapter Eighteen

withstand the barrage of strong winds and snow, I'm planted to where I stand.

The solace I feel should have frightened me. It should have triggered the guilt that's plagued me the past few years. But it never comes. And for the first time in a long while, I can breathe.

I close my eyes and let myself give in to the moment that I seldom have. This euphoria is a high that I'm willing to pay any amount of money for, but even I know this is something money can't buy.

The sound of footsteps takes me out of my musing. Two arms wrap around my hips, meeting on my stomach, followed by soft kisses on the back of my neck.

"It's so beautiful out here," Ash says.

I turn around and with my hands I fix his hair that is sticking up.

"It is, isn't it? I forgot how much I love this place."

He joins me in the blanket that is wrapped round me, and we enjoy the view from the inside.

"Trav?"

"Yeah?"

"I'm really proud of you, and proud of everything you've accomplished these past few years. I just want you to know that."

"Thank you," is all I'm able to say as a lump starts to form in my throat. I tighten my hold on him, and he rests his head on my shoulder.

After a few minutes, Ash heads to the kitchen and starts searching the fridge.

"For someone who is only planning to spend the weekend, you sure brought a lot of food."

"That's called planning, baby. I don't want to be stranded here without food."

"Baby? Since when am I baby? Does that make you my daddy?" he asks, raising his eyebrows and leering back at me.

"I heard it just as it left my lips. Forget I even said that."

"Whatever you say, daddy," Ash jokes.

"Stop it!" I protest, thoroughly enjoying this interaction.

Because Ash didn't bring any clothes suitable for playing outside in the snow, and I know how much he hates being cold, we decide to stay in and play board games instead.

"It would have been much more fun to play strip poker than this boring Scrabble crap," I say as I lose for the third straight time.

"You're such a sore loser," he says as he lays out his tiles that spelled *zymurgy*.

"Is that even a word? I feel like you're taking advantage of my dumbness and the lack of internet connection to check."

"Stop saying that. You are not dumb. You're one of

Chapter Eighteen

the smartest people I know—and I work with brainiacs," he says. I'd forgotten how much he hates it when I put myself down like that.

"I'm sorry, I didn't mean to upset you. But for real though, is that a word?" I stand up and go around the other side of the coffee table to kiss him and ease his brewing irritation. That seems to work when I feel him melt from my touch.

I want so much to stay in this bubble with Ash, but I know we eventually have to leave. We got carried away last night and we haven't even started talking about the implication of this weekend on our relationship. I think it's safe to say we've crossed the line that divides friendship and something completely different. I want to know where Ash stands, but I'm afraid he'll say that last night was a mistake, and I'm even more afraid he'll say it wasn't.

Nothing has changed with my situation. I'm still chained to the secrets and there's only one way this can end. And the idea of hurting Ash again is more than I can bear.

"What's on your mind?" Ash pulls me back from my daydreaming.

"I was just thinking about something."

"Thinking about what?" he asks, slightly pulling away to look me in the eyes. Those blue eyes are begging for answers.

"I was thinking about this," I answer, moving my hand between him and I. "What are we doing?"

"I don't know. But after what happened at the hospital yesterday, all I can think about is you. The thought of not being able to see you, touch you, hear your voice brings so much sorrow that I can't breathe. I know it's silly, because you're here. You're alive. I guess what I'm trying to say is, let's see where this goes. Because I can't remember the last time I was this happy. This could all blow up in our faces, but it's the risk I'm willing to take."

This is a bad idea, but I'm too weak to say no to his offer. "As long as you're sure. Just let me know if it gets to be too much," I say.

"I will."

Chapter Nineteen
Ashton

Instead of driving back home after the weekend in the cabin with Travis, I find myself standing in front of my parents' house. My conversation with him gave me the boost I need to finally confront my relationship with my mom. I've been putting it off since I moved back to Seattle, and I always find an excuse to never follow through. Travis is right. If I'm willing to give him another chance, I should be able to extend my mom the same courtesy.

This conversation has been a long time coming. In fact, it's eight years too late, and if I'm being completely honest, my mom has been the punching bag for everything that has happened to me over the past six years. Because somehow, I know she will always take every hit and every blow. I know that she is my safe place, so I just direct all my frustration and anger toward her.

I still have a key, but decide to ring the doorbell instead. I bite my lower lip and wipe my clammy hands on my jeans and ring the bell one more time. After a couple of rings, Mom opens the door, and a mixture of surprise and unease washes over her face.

"Ash?"

"Hi Mom, I'm sorry to show up unannounced—"

She interrupts me before I finish. "Oh sweetie, no need to apologize. I'm glad you're here. Why didn't you use your key?" she asks as she opens the door wide to let me in. She must have been in the middle of cooking as I get a whiff of sauteed garlic and other aromatic spices.

"I just wanted to talk," I begin.

I follow her to the kitchen and my initial suspicion that she's cooking is confirmed, as a pile of dishes and ingredients, all in different stages of preparation, are scattered over the kitchen island. My mom is an amazing cook but an extremely messy prepper.

"Do you need anything? Your dad isn't home."

"That's okay. I came to talk to you."

She dials the gas stove to low and turns her attention to me. Her hand is playing with the dish towel she used after washing her hands, while she uses her other hand to straighten her already perfect hair. She goes

Chapter Nineteen

to the refrigerator to grab a can of sparkling water I hadn't asked for, and when she returns to the other side of the kitchen island, she looks at me inquisitively.

"I'm sorry I missed all the holidays these past few years," I begin. "I'm sorry that I never pick up when you call, or return your text messages, but most of all, I'm sorry for being a terrible son when all you've done is love and support me."

I feel a drop of water on my hand in my lap. I start to think it's from the can my mom handed me, only I haven't picked it up since I placed it in front of me. I put my hand to my face and realize it's coming from my eyes. I don't know how Mom gets to me so quickly, but the next thing I know, I'm inside her embrace.

"I'm sorry, Mom," I say with a gravelly voice. "I'm so sorry."

"Oh son, I'm sorry too. I never should have done what I did. And not just about Stanford, but for all the meddling I've done to get my way. You're my only baby and I just want what's best for you, and sometimes I get carried away. I'm sorry you doubted yourself. If I made you think that you weren't good enough, then I'm even sorrier. I am so proud of you and I always will be," she says with tears in her eyes.

I pull back from her embrace and look at her face. "I was so mad, and then I went through some personal stuff and I directed all my anger at you and that wasn't fair. You didn't deserve that. I am so sorry. Please don't hate me, Mom."

"I don't hate you, sweetheart. I will never hate you. But I worry about you. You keep everything inside and I can see that you're hurting."

"I'm going to be okay, Mom."

"Your dad and I are here if you need anything. I promise to be better."

"I know. Thank you."

"I love you, sweetheart."

"I love you too, Mom."

After a few more minutes of hugging and getting caught up, Mom goes back to her cooking and I help her clean up the kitchen, which looks like a battlefield.

"Can you stay for dinner?" she asks hesitantly.

"I would love to."

Chapter Twenty
Travis

I stayed in the cabin for a few hours after Ash left so I could put out the fire, clean up, and secure the place for the winter, since I doubted it would get used anytime soon. He offered to help, but I refused, since it was getting dark out and I didn't want him to drive down the snowy mountain in pitch black.

After putting up resistance, I was able to convince him to take off, with a promise that I would call him as soon as I got home.

It's late in the evening when I arrive at my parents' house. The only light visible is the one from their bedroom. Thinking that everyone had already retired for the evening, I slowly and silently make my way inside.

"Hey son, how was your trip?" Not expecting anyone

to be up, I startle when I hear my dad's voice from the living room.

"Jesus, you scared me, Dad!" I say, clutching my chest to cradle my racing heartbeat.

"I'm sorry, buddy. I didn't mean to scare you."

"Don't worry about it. What are you still doing up?"

"It's just one of those nights where I can't seem to fall asleep. I just finished a book." He waves the book in his hand.

"Do you want some company?" It's been a while since we spent time when it's just us. And since I'm not tired and have no plans tomorrow morning, I walk to the living room before he even responds to my question. I stop by the small bar and pour us each a glass of scotch. "On the rocks, please," I hear my dad say.

I plop two cubes of ice in our glasses. "You got it."

After handing him his glass, I sit on the chair opposite his so we are facing each other. The moonlight is penetrating through the large glass picture window, giving the room a cozy feel. Dad takes a sip of his drink and releases a sigh of contentment. This is the first time since I've been home that I'm able to look closely at him. For a man in his sixties, he appears quite youthful. He carries himself well, and he always has a smile on his face. Even now, just sitting here with me doing nothing but staring at each other, he's smiling.

Chapter Twenty

"You know, Dad, what you and Mom have is truly remarkable." If he is surprised by the statement and the direction this chitchat is going, he doesn't show it. Instead, he indulges me.

"It is. It's not every day that you find and marry your best friend, soulmate, and partner. And to fall in love with each other, it is truly magical."

"I wish I could be that lucky," I admit.

"How was your trip to the cabin?"

"I had a great time. It brought back a lot of fond memories. Ash even showed up unexpectedly."

"He did, huh? You and Ash always pick up right where you leave off. Did he enjoy the trip to the mountains too?"

"Yes. We had an amazing time. It's good for him to take a break once in a while. He's always either studying or working. Never any time for play."

"That's good to hear. He's a very special kid."

"Dad, he's hardly a kid anymore," I joke.

"Don't I know it. Looking at you two makes me feel old. I remember when you were kids. You were inseparable. One wouldn't do something without the other. When you guys were teenagers, Olivia, Preston, your mom and I had to be on our toes. You two were too clever and smart for your own good."

"We weren't that bad, were we?"

"Nah, you're right, you guys were good kids."

I take a sip of scotch and nod in agreement, thinking about our teenage years.

"What happened between the two of you?" Dad asks unexpectedly.

"What do you mean?" I say, trying to stall the conversation so I can come up with a different lie than the one I usually tell. I don't know why, but it's been harder and harder to deceive those around me, especially those that I love. Afraid of what I will see on my father's face, I lift the glass of scotch and swirl it around before taking another sip.

"Look, Travis, I don't want to make you uncomfortable—and please tell me if I'm overstepping here—but I feel you two are strained now." I can feel his gaze on me, and I'm too much of a coward to look him in the eyes.

"You and Ash were always together. And then all of a sudden, he stopped coming home, even when you were back in town during your seasons."

I begin to squirm in my chair, feeling like a trapped animal.

"Whatever it was that happened between you two, we can tell there was a change in you boys."

"Dad, I'm sorry. We didn't mean to worry you. It was just complicated." The word *complicated* comes out of me like a well-rehearsed line. Because it is. I've said that same phrase more times than I care to remember.

Chapter Twenty

My answer is met with silence, and I find him studying me. "That's the most I'll get from you, isn't it?" he says, sounding disappointed.

I don't say anything. I just sit here. I want to tell him the truth so badly. To finally let him know what I've been hiding for the past ten years, but I just don't know how. I have gotten so good at hiding this part of me for so long that it's all I've ever known. I know that my secret is safe with them, but I think the fear of disappointing them is preventing me from coming out.

I wish I had Ash's courage at this very moment. Coming out for him came naturally, and the support he received from his family was so amazing, and I hate that I question how my own family will react.

I don't know how long I've been sitting quietly with my thoughts when I hear him get up. He grabs both of our empty glasses.

"Dad..." I'm not able to say anything more when an uncontrollable sob escapes my mouth. He quickly sets the glasses down and rushes toward me. He sits on the edge of the coffee table between us so we're face-to-face. I lower my chin to my chest as more tears flow.

"It's okay, son, let it out," I hear him say softly as he rubs my back, trying to console me.

"I'm sorry, Dad. I don't know how do to this. I'm such a coward."

"It's okay, Travis. You don't have to tell me anything you're not prepared to."

He's probably the most understanding father anyone could ask for, and I can't believe I ever doubt him or my mom. I take a long, slow breath, and raise my head to look directly at him.

"Dad, I'm gay."

My declaration is met with silence and fear envelops my whole body. All my fears arrive at once and they overcome my emotions. I continue to watch my dad for a reaction when I see a grin come over his face.

Confused, I ask, "Why are you smiling? Did you hear what I said? I'm *gay*."

"I hear you." Still grinning, he starts laughing. I hear shuffling and sniffling from across the room and discover my mom standing there, crying. And with the same smile on her face, I know they're tears of joy. She joins us and pulls me in for a loving hug.

"I am so proud of you, son," she says.

Finally catching on to what's happening, I ask, "Wait, did you guys know?"

My parents look at each other and smile. My mom speaks first.

"Sweetie, the way you look at Ash and how your face lights up when he is around, how could we not know?" she says.

"We were just waiting for you to tell us. We were

Chapter Twenty

actually surprised that you didn't when Ash came out at fifteen," Dad continues.

"Why didn't you?" my mom asks, and just like that, the cloud over me is back. Mom senses my internal battle and says, "I'm sure you have your reasons, love."

"Can I ask you to keep it to yourselves for now?" I can see their confusion, but they both nod in understanding of my request.

I tell Mom and Dad everything about my relationship with Ash up until our breakup six years ago. They ask why we broke up and I tell them it was because Ash didn't want to be with someone who was in the closet, and I wasn't ready to come out.

"Oh my gosh, I cannot believe how late it is," my mom says, peeking at her watch. "We'd better call it a night."

We kiss each other goodnight and make our way upstairs. Before going to our bedrooms, my father takes a moment and says, "I am so proud of you, son. It takes guts to do what you just did. Thank you for opening up to your mom and I. You're no coward, and we love you very much."

"I know, Dad. Thank you."

Chapter Twenty-One
Ashton

My black-and-white life suddenly turned technicolor after my weekend with Travis. We haven't labeled our relationship, but we're both in agreement that we will cherish whatever time we have together. Honestly, I'm okay with that. Travis and I had a great relationship until we gave it a label of boyfriends. Everything after that was just more and more problems. Maybe it will be different this time.

"Ash!" Katie calls as I enter the elevator heading up to the residents' locker room. I use my leg to keep the door open as she rushes inside.

"Good morning," I say, only to find her giving me a knowing look.

"What?"

Chapter Twenty-One

"You got laid, didn't you? Something's different about you." She surveys my face.

"Different how?" I ask.

"Well, for starters, you're smiling."

"Hey, I smile," I say defensively.

"Easy queen, I'm not saying it's bad. I actually kinda like it."

"What did you just call me?" I ask, trying to prevent my smile from turning into a grin.

"Queen," Katie repeats.

"I don't think you're allowed to call gay guys queen."

"I didn't call *them* queen, I called *you* queen."

I'm about to argue with her when the elevator opens on the second floor and Dr. Kirkland enters. I haven't seen him since last Friday and my plan today was to find him and thank him for supporting me.

"Dr. Kennedy, how are you doing?" he asks, sincerity on his face.

"I'm doing a lot better, thank you," I answer. "I don't know what I would have done without your help. Thanks again, Dr. Kirkland."

It still breaks my heart whenever I think about that evening, but like what Dr. Kirkland and Katie said, we'd done everything we could to save the patient's life. In the end, it just wasn't enough.

"I'm glad to hear that," he says as the elevator opens at our floor.

Katie and I continue to walk toward our locker room, and immediately pick up where we left off.

"So, back to you," she purrs. "Where did you go?"

"I went to a friend's cabin by Mount Rainier."

"Alone?" she questions.

"Katie, let's not do this right now. We're going to be late for rounds."

"Why do I have a feeling that there's something you're not telling me?" she says, and I roll my eyes at her. Because duh, it doesn't take a brain surgeon to figure that one out."

"I'll talk to you later, okay," I plead.

"Promise?"

"Yes, I promise."

The morning rounds are uneventful, which I appreciate. We follow our attendings as we see the patients who are recovering from surgery in the days prior, and the ones who have been in hospital for a while for surveillance. As usual, the attendings ask us questions while we try to impress them by giving the best answers, hoping we get picked for their next interesting case.

It's still early when we finish, and Katie is already at my side, like a dog on a bone, trying to get the details of my weekend away.

"You're something else," I say as I shake my head.

"Hey, you owe me this."

Chapter Twenty-One

"How do you figure?"

"Come on, Ash, you're killing me. Can you just please tell me?"

"I like you better when you're all serious," I complain.

"No, you don't. Now spill the tea," she demands.

"Spill the tea? Since when do you speak gay?" I ask.

"Since forever! I am a fierce ally of the community, in case it matters."

I'm learning just how lucky I am to have a friend like her. I want to tell her everything, but how can I without complicating things with Travis?

"You get to ask one question and that's it. You'd better pick wisely," I say.

"Who'd you go with?" Damn! She picked a good one.

"I went with someone from high school. He and I had a thing that never really went anywhere. He's back in town so...we're just having fun," I say. It's the truth, sans specific details.

"So, what's his name?" she follows up.

"One question, remember?"

"Oh, not fair," she protests. The pout she is sporting is so comical, that it makes me laugh. "I don't care who he is, but if he can make you grin like that, I'm all for it."

Lunch time comes and my excitement is off the chain. I've been trying to find an opportunity to call Travis, but every time I do, I get paged.

"Hi, I was hoping you'd call," Travis says when I finally manage it.

"It's been busy."

"Do you have any plans tonight?"

"No," I answer, hoping that my excitement isn't too obvious.

"Great! I was hoping to take you out for dinner tonight."

"I have a better idea. How about we stay in at my place. I can make us something for dinner and you haven't even seen my houseboat yet."

"Is this a ploy to get into my pants?"

"Maybe I was just thinking that it'll be better so you don't have to constantly worry about the paparazzi and fans. But going out is fine too." I finally stop my rambling.

"Ash, I'm kidding! I love your plan. What time do you get off?

"I'll be done by five so maybe come over at seven o'clock? I'll text you the address."

"That's perfect. See you tonight. I'll bring the wine."

"Okay. See ya. Bye."

The rest of my shift drags on, and I can't contain my excitement about this evening. It's been on my mind since my conversation with Travis and I've been giddy all day.

I play soft music in the background while I light

Chapter Twenty-One

some candles, placing one of them in the center of the table and a couple on the counter top. I change the setting of the lights to dim, which softens the interior so we can enjoy the incredible city views.

There's a knock on the door. I glance in the mirror one last time before I head over to let Travis in. He looks like a god leaning on the frame of the door, wearing a black shirt with the top three buttons undone. The tight shirt is tucked into a pair of dark denim jeans that hug every muscle in his thighs and legs. The outfit is finished with a pair of dark leather chukka boots.

"Are you done?" he says. I look up and his wicked smile isn't trying to hide his enjoyment of my perusal.

"What?" I ask as I try to hide the embarrassment of being caught checking him out again. He just laughs and I let him in. The moment I have the door closed, he grabs my waist and kisses me for all I'm worth. He tastes like mint and raspberry from chewing his favorite gum, and the scent of his cologne is putting a spell on my senses.

"I missed you today," Travis says as soon as he lets go of my lips. He walks farther into the houseboat and looks around, taking in the view of the lake and the city in front of us.

"This place is nice," he says, while adding a low whistle.

My friend Dawson bought this place at an auction after the original owner defaulted. I remembered him showing me old photos of how this place looked before he started renovating it a couple of years ago. His talent in restoring old homes is something I admire about him. And doing it all alone makes it even more remarkable.

"This is Dawson's?" He turns around and looks at me. "Is he here?" Travis has always been jealous of Dawson, and the look of jealousy on his face makes me want to have a little fun.

"Yeah, he's in my room if you want to say hi. Actually, let me get him. Baby, can you come out? Travis is here," I call out as I walk toward the hallway.

"What the fuck, Ash? You're with fucking Dawson? You said you've never been with anyone else." He turns red as he paces the room and curls his hands into fists. His nostrils flare and it takes everything in me to not laugh, but when I can no longer hold it in, I burst out into fits of laughter.

"Oh, you little fucker," he says, walking toward me with a look that says *you're going to get it*. He reaches me and starts kissing me passionately, but the kisses are awkward since I can't stop laughing. He pins me to the wall.

"I hope you're hungry," I ask in between his kisses and my laughs.

Chapter Twenty-One

"Oh, I'm hungry alright." His suggestive tone makes me believe that he isn't referring to dinner but something entirely different. "You think you can just tease me like that and get away with it?"

"As much as I want to jump your bones right now, we have to eat dinner first," I say as I pull away from him and adjust my pants, then walk away to check the oven for our dinner.

"I see that," he teases, sounding proud of what his touch does to me.

After telling Travis which cabinets the plates and silverware are located in, he helps set the dining table. I pour two glasses of chardonnay and hand one to him.

The oven timer dings, and the smell of roasted chicken and vegetables fills the room as I open it.

Our dinner is mostly filled with catching up on our days since the cabin. I let Travis know that I had stopped by my parents' house and had the opportunity to speak with my mom about how things had been. I thanked him for encouraging me to bridge the gap that existed between us, and assured him we were moving forward on much better terms.

"Who knew you were such a good cook?" Travis says.

"Well, I have had a lot of practice these past several years," I answer.

"I can see that. It was delicious. I could get used to that really easy."

"I'm a doctor, remember? There won't be a lot of this in our future."

Chapter Twenty-Two
Ashton

After dinner, Travis helps me clean up the kitchen, and then we relax on the oversized leather couch. We both marvel at the stunning view of the Space Needle, and I stand up and grab both of our wine glasses.

"Whoa, mister, where do you think you're going?" Travis asks.

"I'm bored of this view." I wave a passing hand at the giant glass doors, feigning a yawn.

"Seriously?" Travis responds. "This million-dollar view is boring you?"

"Seen it, done that. I was hoping to catch a better view from that side of the houseboat." I point to the back of the house where my bedroom is.

"The side facing your neighbor and the street?" He has a confused look on his face.

I head to the kitchen, rinse out our glasses, and uncork another bottle of wine.

"Is that for me?" Travis has snuck up behind me and places his hands on my hips.

"Oh! Look who figured things out, and all on his very own," I tease.

"Whatever, brainiac. Us jocks require a more upfront, easy-to-read hint than you give."

"Would you have preferred me shaking my ass directly in your face?" I ask.

"Well, I would have gotten the hint a lot quicker." Travis reaches around and brings my hand back to his crotch. "No hint needed for Junior, though."

I turn around and face him, and he pulls me tightly into him. I love being in Travis' arms, and I look around the houseboat thinking about how I would love to spend all my days doing this with him. Coming home from the hospital when he's off tour to find him curled up waiting for me. We would make love, prep our dinners together, and live a relaxed, fulfilled life as a happy couple.

"Where'd you go, handsome?" Travis brings me back from my 1950s sitcom fantasy.

"Mmmm, I'm right here, stud." I slide my hand back to his erection. "Follow me. Grab the bottle too, this could be a while." I wink seductively at him and head toward the bedroom.

Chapter Twenty-Two

"Wait for me, you cock tease. No viewing party starts without the star."

I unbutton my dress shirt and drop it when I'm halfway down the hall on my way to the bedroom. After I hear it land lightly behind me, I reach my foot back for it and kick it back at Travis. I turn my head to make sure he's on his way and move my eyes down to floor as if to say, *Pick that up.*

"Whoa! Dinner and a show?" he laughs.

Travis is about ten to twelve feet behind me as I saunter down the hallway. My bare feet make no sound as I glide to the bedroom. I reach the door to my bedroom and stop suddenly. I hear no noise, so I know he has stopped as well. For dramatic effect, I stand motionless for several seconds. The only noise is the lapping of water against the outdoor deck edge, and some seriously heavy breathing coming from him.

Moving slowly, I bring my hands down from the insides of the bedroom door where they had been while I posed. I make a big show of unzipping my jeans very slowly, to make sure the sound of the zipper sliding down, one tooth at a time, is obvious. Knowing that I have no underwear on is making me hot, and I know he's going to enjoy what I do next.

I let my jeans fall to the floor and do not make a single move. I'm standing in the doorway with my jeans pooled around my ankles and my bare ass on full display. I hear two steps come closer and what I think is a piece of clothing hitting the floor behind me. I don't move. Two more steps creep forward and then nothing but silence. I can hear the effort being spent through Travis' breathing as he removes his boot. Clunk. A moment later another boot. Clunk. I'm still motionless when I hear the familiar sound of a zipper going down. Three, maybe four seconds go by, and I hear the whoosh of clothing being kicked in my direction. I look down to my feet and see Travis' jeans land alongside my feet. A moment later a pair of boxers hit the back of my leg. Someone else is naked.

I still don't move an inch when I hear his steps closing in. The steps are soft as his bare feet gently slide across the hallway hardwoods. Travis comes up behind me, not touching me. I can hear his breath and I feel his foot brush against my legs as he steps on my bundle of jeans and presses his foot down on them.

"Step out of them, Ash," he moans.

I do as I'm told, and release my feet one by one. He still has not touched me. Travis drags the jeans back away from my feet and out of his way. My skin tightens and tingles in anticipation of his touch.

"You're right. The view is better on this side of the house." His voice is low and steady.

Travis puts his foot between my feet and taps the inside of my ankle, urging me to spread them apart.

Chapter Twenty-Two

"Mmmm, this view just keeps getting better and better."

A palm gently presses against one of my ass cheeks as Travis begins to squeeze and massage it. He lifts it up and lets it drop with a firm bounce. Another palm grabs the other cheek, and he moves forward. I feel his skin touch mine, and his erect cock is making its way between my ass cheeks. He lifts them higher and apart so he can wedge himself inside them. I lay my head back on his chest and he reaches around my hips to discover my fully attentive erection waiting for him.

"Do all the houses come with this view?"

I break my silence and breathlessly say, "This one does, and it gets even better over there." I gently move my head to motion toward the bed.

Travis pushes me forward and steers me toward it. "Lie on your stomach," he whispers.

Travis manages to hold me as he lays me gently on the bed. His erection is still hard and wedged between my legs as he brings himself down on top of me.

"You feel so good, baby. I hate to break the mood, but I would rather not spit on my cock tonight," he teases.

A wave of excitement runs through my body in anticipation. I reach across to the nightstand, pull open the drawer and grab the bottle of lube.

"I thought you might be trying to take advantage of my hospitality tonight," I say, laying the lube next to him.

"I'm only here for the view. This was your idea, remember? It wasn't me that was putting on that little show in the hall."

"How about less talk and more observation of this view," I growl back as I raise my hips off the bed. "Do you need an embossed invitation or is this going to work?"

I hear Travis pop the lid off the lube bottle as he removes his cock from between my legs.

"My cock is only going to be gone a second. I hope you can wait that long."

I decide to reach back with both hands and pull my ass cheeks apart so he can see my welcoming hole.

"In case you forgot your way, big boy," I tease.

"Whatever you pay for the view around here, you're not paying enough," Travis' deep voice moans in my ear as I feel the first hint of pressure.

I relax my entire body as Travis holds my hands above my head and we intertwine our fingers tightly. He slowly moves inside me. I give a little and he takes a little more until he's fully in me.

Travis has his mouth against my ear as he grinds into me and he breathes heavily with pleasure. I'm fully exposed to him and welcome him into my body. The pleasure of having him inside me is intoxicating, and the joy I feel being with him like this has my heart swelling.

"This feel good, baby?" he asks.

"Oh yeah. I love having you inside me."

Travis is moaning as he continues to grind his hips into me. We're both holding the other's hands tight as we gently move as one. Our love is slow, deliberate, and passionate. Neither of us is in a hurry. The pressure of his weight on my back is amazing and I arch my ass back into him, begging him to fill me up. Travis increases his motions as he dives deeper with each thrust, and holds it there before gently pulling his entire length out again. My own erection is rubbing against the comforter in rhythm with his thrusts and I can feel my orgasm building as we ride wave after wave of sensation.

"I'm close, Trav." I grit my teeth as I release my words.

Travis grabs my hips and pulls me up and onto my knees as he stands on the floor near the edge of the bed. His rhythm is getting faster and more aggressive. I hear his deep moans and know that he's also building toward his climax.

"Fuck, Ash! You're so hot, baby." He's pounding hard now, his hands gripping my hips tighter.

I push my ass back against his pounding and start pleasuring myself. I know he's close because his breathing is hard, like he's running that last ten yards of a 50-yard sprint.

"Don't stop, Trav! Keep going!" I'm rocking back and forth, riding him as hard as he's delivering it to me.

"Ash, this is amazing. I fucking love your ass, baby."

I know he's about to blow his load because he's getting wilder and more feverish with his efforts.

"Come on, baby, come on." I'm moaning loud as my face is flat on the bed, tossing back and forth in delirium. I feel my load charging up for release and welcome the convulsions as I jack my cock harder and shoot all over the sheets. "Travis!" I yell as my release continues to pump out of my balls.

Travis slams into me and forces me flat onto the bed as he releases his orgasm deep inside me.

"Oh my god! Ash, that was amazing, baby." He groans, flexing his cock and pumping out the last bit of his orgasm. "Wow, you're amazing."

I'm panting and spent. My body wracks with shivers from my own explosion and the amazing love-making we just shared.

"That was amazing, Trav. I love you." I say the words before thinking about their implications. Damn it.

Chapter Twenty-Three
Travis

It's a whisper, but I hear it, and the look of shock on Ash's face when he realizes he's said those three words out loud assures me that my mind didn't make it up. Ash loves me. My stomach drops from the admission, not because I don't believe him, but because I do, and the scarier part is, I love him too. I always have, and I always will.

But this cannot happen. Not again.

I shake my head frantically as I quickly get up and search for my underwear that I had kicked off in the hallway. I slightly lose my balance while I pull them on, but I manage to find purchase on the wall with my shaky hand.

I can feel him watching me, but I don't dare return his stare, afraid of what I will find in his eyes.

I can't believe I let this happen again, that I'm hurting him again. Fuck!

"Trav," he says. The fear of hurting him again is so paralyzing that I can't do anything but stare back. Ash slowly heads in my direction until he's standing in front of me.

"Trav, it's okay. Forget what I said. I didn't mean it. It was the heat of the moment. Orgasms make me say crazy stuff. Let's go back to bed," he says, but his eyes say otherwise. He follows his statement with a nervous laugh. I'm not even sure if he buys his lame excuse since he starts biting his lower lip, his telltale sign.

"Ash. We can't—"

"Sure we can, come on. It's no big deal. Let's forget what I said and get back in bed. All will be well in the morning."

I look around for the rest of my clothes that are strewn along the hallway and put them on piece by piece.

"I have to go," I say, making my way toward the door.

"So, you're just going to leave? You won't even talk about it?" He follows me down the hall and places himself in front of the door, making it impossible for me to leave.

"This is what I was afraid would happen. This is six years ago all over again. I'm sorry, Ash. I have to go."

Chapter Twenty-Three

Ash hugs me the moment I get close to him. I hug him back, knowing this will be the last time I will ever touch this man. I embed the feel of him in my mind for when I have to relive this moment. Once again, I'm saying goodbye to the man of my dreams and the love of my life. Only this time, I know it's the absolute last. It has to be. I peel his arms away one at a time, and with a heavy heart I let him go.

"Goodbye, Ash. I'm so sorry."

Too shaky to drive, I pull over in one of the city parks where I let go of all the emotion I've been keeping inside. I slam my steering wheel dozens of times, hoping the pain will dull the ache of my breaking heart. I scream at the top of my lungs until my body punishes me with a burning in my chest.

I want to believe that I can do it, that I can be with him and take what Ash is offering, but I know I'm only going to prolong the inevitable. This was always how it was going to end. We were just kidding ourselves when we thought it would be different this time. Fuck. Fuck. Fuck!

I grab my phone from the center console, where I put it before my evening with Ash.

I tap my phone to life and hit Aaliyah's contact.

"Travis?" Aaliyah answers in the middle of a yawn. I hadn't even bothered to remember the time difference between the East Coast and West Coast. I glance at the clock on the dashboard and find it's past nine, which means past midnight in New York City. "Travis, are you still there? Did you drunk dial me?"

"No. I wish I was drunk. I'm sorry to wake you, but do you think you can get me a flight back to New York?"

"When?"

"Tonight."

"What? Travis, it's midnight. Is everything okay?"

"It's only nine o'clock here," I say.

"What's going on? What the hell happened since we spoke a couple of hours ago?" she asks in confusion.

"Can you get me out of here or what?"

My last question is followed by momentary silence, but she eventually agrees to help me.

I manage to drive home with the little strength I have left.

"Travis, is that you?" I hear my mom call from the living room as I make my way upstairs.

"Yeah, it's me. I'm heading to my room."

"How was your dinner with Ash, honey?" She must have heard stress in my voice. "What's wrong, son? Have you been crying? What happened?"

"I'm heading back to New York tonight, Mom. Something just came up." Another lie.

"But it's late. Is Ash okay? Can't you wait until tomorrow?" She continues asking questions and just the mention of Ash's name makes me want to vomit from all the guilt I'm bearing because of my stupidity.

"He's fine, Mom, everything is going to be fine. I just need to get back to New York today, okay?"

She's not buying it. "Sweetie, what's going on with you?"

"Nothing, I just need to go." I don't wait for her to say anything else as I run up to my room so I can pack up my shit and get out of here. I see my dad heading out of his room when I reach the hallway. I ignore his calls as I step into my room and shut the door. I take a calming breath and lean back on it.

It doesn't take me long to pack all my things. And, as expected, both my parents are waiting for me when I get downstairs. My dad is about to say something when I interrupt him.

"Dad, I just need to go."

"Okay, I'll drive you to the airport," he says.

"I can take an Uber."

"Travis James Montgomery, I am driving you to the airport." He only calls me by my full name when I'm in trouble, and even though I'm a grown-ass man, I still respect my parents enough not to argue.

"Fine."

I kiss Mom goodbye and give her one last apology. Dad is already waiting for me in the car when I get outside.

Even though I thought he would have a slew of questions for me, he stays quiet as we make our way to the airport. This is the trick he used on me when I was younger and in trouble. And, just like then, it's still effective because I'm the one who speaks first.

"I know you have a lot of questions, but I just can't deal with it right now," I say, breaking the silence.

"Travis, aren't you tired of always running away from Ash? How long are you going to keep doing this?" His question is meant to be rhetorical, which is a good thing because I don't have an answer for him. "Just know one thing, Travis. We're always here for you."

All I'm capable of saying in return is, "Thank you, Dad."

Chapter Twenty-Four
Ashton

Is there a statute of limitations for waiting on something that will never come to fruition? Because if there is, I would really like it to be now.

My insatiable appetite for disappointment and pain where Travis is concerned is so consuming that I'm willing to take how little he can give me just to tide me over until the next time. Like a junkie waiting for his next fix.

There's a part of me that anticipated this ending, but I was willing to try. I'm tired of being lonely and sad, so I went against my better judgment and persuaded him to give us one last shot, this time without any expectations, but it wasn't enough.

It's been hours since Travis left my place in a hurry and I'm still sitting in the same spot, shell-shocked, wishing he would come back. But he doesn't, just like the way it was when he left six years ago. I didn't mean to say *I love you* out loud, but it's exactly what I felt. I tried to play it off by assuring him that I didn't mean it, but my reasons weren't even convincing for me, let alone for Travis.

I force myself off the sofa and into the kitchen to look for anything that is stronger than wine. I find an unopened bottle of vodka that Katie had given me as a housewarming gift when I moved in a couple of months ago. I grab a glass out of the cabinet and pour a generous amount, without bothering to put in ice or soda. I gulp the liquor down and continue my pity party.

Why won't he choose me? Why does it have to be either me or tennis? Why can't those two things exist together in his world?

I ask myself the same questions over and over again, wishing each time that the answers would be different. I can't believe I let myself back into this mess. And for what—so I could be with him knowing that it's temporary? So I could satisfy the need I've deprived myself? Because for so long I only believed that Travis could fill that need?

When will I learn my lesson? Will I ever learn? How long do I have to wait before I demand the best for myself? How much longer do I have to keep banging

Chapter Twenty-Four

my head on the same wall before I realize he will never give me what I want?

I down another glass of vodka to try to ease the pain that is boring another hole in my soul, but the burn of alcohol never reaches the ache in my heart, so another one immediately follows.

The instinct to blame myself kicks in, along with the desire to isolate myself from the world, but that didn't help me then and it will not help me now. I tend to keep people at arm's length, but not anymore. I dial the number of the one person I know will understand.

"Ash, what's going on?" Katie answers after a few rings.

I glance at the screen and feel guilty for bothering my friend at two o'clock in the morning. "Oh, Katie. I'm so sorry. I didn't realize it's this late. I'll call you tomorrow." I get ready to hang up, but I hear her yell so I stay on the line.

"Ash, wait! Don't hang up. What's wrong?"

My heart is lodged in my throat and it prevents me from answering her question, but it doesn't prevent a sob from escaping. Katie lets me cry without saying anything. Minutes pass.

I hear a knock on my door that sobers me up a little, since I'm not expecting anyone this late. Could it be Travis? "Hold on for a second, Katie. There's someone at the door."

I look out the peephole and when I see who is on the other side, I'm dumbfounded. "How? What? How did you do that?"

I pull Katie inside as my legs go weak underneath me, and I hug her as if she's my lifeline. I need her to prevent me from drowning in my sorrow, and just when I think my tears have run dry, I weep uncontrollably.

"Shh. It's okay. I'm here," she says, rubbing my back.

"I'm sorry I called you this late," I'm finally able say after my sobbing subsides.

"I'm glad you did, Ash."

"How did you get here that fast? You live twenty minutes away."

"I had a trauma consult that came into the ER and I was headed home when you called. I'm glad I was close by."

We sit down on the same sofa I had been on the past few hours and she faces me. Holding my hand, she looks me in the eye and wipes away stray tears from my cheeks. Noticing my hair is a mess, she attempts to straighten it. The tenderness of her touch gives me temporary reprieve from my aching heart.

"Wanna talk about it?" she asks.

I nod my head and tell her everything about Travis. I begin from when we were teenagers and end by telling her about him walking out earlier.

Chapter Twenty-Four

Katie listens without judgment. "What are you going to do now?" she asks.

"I don't know yet. But one thing I know for sure, I need to move on with my life."

"Are you sure that's what you want to do?"

"I do, I really do," I answer with a determined nod.

"Then I'm here for you," she says as she puts her hand over mine.

I wake up because the sunlight is streaming through my bedroom window and curse myself for not having the smarts to close the blinds before going to bed. But after my 'Come to Jesus' session with Katie, I didn't have any smarts to do anything but go to bed. It takes a minute for my eyes to adjust to the brightness of my room, and when I sit up I almost vomit. I feel like my head is being split open with a dull ax and can feel my pulse beating angrily in my temples.

"I'm not drinking ever again," I groan.

I go to the bathroom to splash water on my face in the hope I can relieve some of my discomfort. I finish my morning routine, put on my robe, and come out of my room to get a pot of coffee started, but am surprised when I see Katie standing in the kitchen staring at the view.

"You have a phenomenal view, Ash," she says without turning around.

"You spent the night? Where did you sleep?"

"The couch. You really need to get your spare bedroom set up. Coffee?" she asks, turning around to grab me a cup.

"Yes. Please." Katie hands me a cup, skipping the cream and sugar since we both like our coffee black.

"I can't believe that you hid all that craziness from me all these years." She doesn't sound upset or bitter about it though.

"It wasn't my secret to tell, Katie. I didn't know how to let you in without outing him," I explain.

"I get that. But I can't wrap my mind around Travis Montgomery being gay. That is huge news."

"Well, he is. He won't be my problem anymore though. I meant what I said last night. I'm moving on. This has gone on way too long."

"Are you sure that's what you want to do?" she asks, looking into my eyes. "I don't know anything about Travis other than what you've told me, but it sounds like he genuinely cares for you. And actually, I think that he loves you too. Why do you think he's never been linked to any women out there?"

"How about because he's gay?" I answer.

"I know that, Ash. But famous people who hide their true selves use other people to convince the public about their charade and to silence any suspicions. Trust me, with his looks and status, he could easily

Chapter Twenty-Four

have an endless list of women to choose from. But why do you think he never went that route?" I finally connect the dots of her train of thought.

"I don't know, Katie," I say while trying to deny the growing optimism that makes me uneasy yet hopeful.

"He didn't do any of that because he knew it would hurt you. He didn't want to hurt you more than he already had. You know I'm on your side, Ash. Always. I just want you to be sure that cutting him out of your life is what you really want to do. And if it is, then I will be the first one to set you up on a date."

We don't speak after that. We enjoy the view in front of us while finishing our cups of coffee. My mind is racing a hundred miles per hour after what Katie just said. I stand up and she follows my move. I look at her and open my mouth to speak when she says, "Go ahead, pack."

Chapter Twenty-Five
Travis

Aaliyah is standing on the curb when I come out of LaGuardia Airport. I sigh, long and deep, as I don't have the energy or patience to deal with anyone right now. Her thumbs are moving swiftly as she types on her cellphone while having a conversation with someone via her Bluetooth headset. Leave it to Aaliyah to manage two conversations at once—and I'm about to be her third.

I close the distance between us, and when she looks up in my direction, she wraps up her conversation.

"Listen, I have to go. Travis is here," Aaliyah tells the person on the other line.

"What's the crisis?" she asks after hanging up the phone.

I hadn't been expecting her to pick me up when I

Chapter Twenty-Five

called last night about my change of plans. She didn't question me when I asked her to make some last-minute arrangements to head back to New York City, but I should have known better. I should have known an interrogation would be waiting for me the moment I landed.

"What crisis? There's no crisis," I quip as I open the trunk of the car and load my luggage. Still trying to ignore her question, I check for oncoming cars before walking around to the driver's side back seat to get in. I recognize the same driver from the last trip, so I tap him on his shoulder and he acknowledges me with a smile.

"Then what's with the sudden trip back to New York? And you look like shit, by the way." The grilling continues the moment she gets inside the car.

"Geez, thanks. You didn't have to pick me up though. You could have just sent the car for me." I hope she can sense the irritation in my voice. I don't know how much I can handle today before I lash out at the next person, and the likelihood of that person being Aaliyah is getting higher.

"You didn't answer my question. What's going on?"

"Aaliyah, nothing is wrong. Jesus Christ! Why is everyone asking me that?" I've never been known for having a temper, but all I need is to be left alone.

Aaliyah flinches and our driver gives me a quick

glance in the rear-view mirror. I slouch down in my seat and place my hand on my forehead, massaging the throbbing headache that has been living there since I left Seattle, since I left Ash. He is never going to forgive me. I know this without a shadow of a doubt. And I deserve it.

"It's been a long night and I'm tired. Can we talk later?" I whisper.

"Okay."

"I'm sorry for being an ass."

"That you are, but we'll talk later."

Aaliyah turns and focuses her attention outside the car, and I do the same. The car's ventilation and the constant hum of passing cars are the only audible sounds. Neither of us utters a word on the ride back to the city, and our driver puts on soft music to break the tension that continues to build inside the confined space. As if the universe finally takes pity on me, we hit every green light on our way to my building.

The silence that greets me in my apartment is deafening, even though that's how it's always been. The light coming from outside doesn't brighten the gloomy gray room, and the dark furniture only makes me feel more depressed. A stark contrast of the past few days at home with my parents and with Ash.

I drop my bags on the floor and go straight to my bedroom. My cold, dark bedroom.

Chapter Twenty-Five

The grumbling of my stomach wakes me from my sleep the following day, and with my resolve to stay in bed stronger than my hunger, I don't get up. The illuminated screen of my cellphone is the only light inside.

My phone buzzes repeatedly, interrupting my sleep. I have no idea what day it is, let alone the time. I've only left my bed to go to the bathroom, and even that is few and far between since I haven't drunk or eaten anything since I arrived.

The buzzing is persistent, so there is only one person this could be. I debate whether or not to ignore the call, but knowing Aaliyah, she'll keep trying until I answer. One glance at the screen confirms my speculation.

"Travis, what's going on? I haven't heard from you in two days," Aaliyah says even before I say anything.

"I'm fine. I can't talk right now," I say.

"Have you seen the news?" she asks.

"No, since when do I watch the news?"

"Trust me, Travis, you want to see this one."

"I can't do this right now. Talk to you later." My frustration is growing by the second.

"Travis, wait! I'm sending you a link. You have to check it out."

My curiosity and paranoia grow at Aaliyah's insistence. Is the news about me? Did someone catch

Ash and I and sell it to the media? I hesitate for a second before asking.

"What is it, Aaliyah? Is it about me?"

"What? No. Why, is there something I should know?" Concern is obvious in her voice.

"No. just send me the link and I'll watch. I have to go."

"And Travis, I'm coming over to your place whether you like it or not." I hang up because I know that arguing will not stop her.

I open the email app on my phone and it only takes me a minute to sign into my account. Sure enough, the item in my inbox is an urgent message from Aaliyah with the subject *YOU WILL NOT BELIEVE THIS*. I click the link that directs me to a YouTube account. Not just any account. It's Evan St. John's YouTube channel. He's a tennis legend and my personal hero. He also served as our team's mentor back in college, and he's given me plenty of personal and professional advice throughout the years.

The video was posted about an hour earlier, and it's already amassed more than a million views and thousands of comments. I'm tempted to scroll through some of the comments, but my curiosity about the content of the video wins. I press play and an image of a serious Evan sitting in what appears to be his home living room appears on screen. This is a complete

Chapter Twenty-Five

departure from the happy-go-lucky guy who can charm anyone with just his smile.

I've followed Evan's career since I was ten years old, and meeting him in person when I was sixteen changed how I viewed the game and how I chose to live the personal side of my life. He's given me the best advice on how to focus and silence all the external factors and distractions that can derail my path to success. I even told Evan at a tennis academy event that I was gay, and he strongly encouraged me to keep that information to myself. His advice has been my mantra ever since, and has brought me to where I am today.

I press play, and no one could have prepared me for what I witness. I slam the laptop closed and throw it on the floor, fuming about what I just watched. I get out of bed, put on a baseball cap and rush out of my apartment.

Arriving at Evan's brownstone, I bang on his door hard enough to rattle the chains on the other side, oblivious to the flashes of paparazzi cameras behind me. I should've known those scandal-hungry opportunists would be here trying to cash in on another salacious story. However, I'm determined to confront him.

Evan opens the door, looking perturbed by the disturbance, and I push my way past him once he acknowledges that I'm the one causing all the noise.

"You fucker! You're a fucking fraud, Evan. I can't believe I listened to you all these years. Why now, huh? Why fucking now?" My anger is off the charts as I pace back and forth in his living room, fuming about his betrayal. "You told me that being openly gay would stop me from achieving any of the goals that I set for myself. You told me to hide who I was because it would only hinder my success. I fucking listened to you! I looked up to you. Oh my god. I broke the love of my life's heart twice because of what you said, and only to find out that you're also gay. And I didn't get the news from you, I heard about it on the fucking internet. How dare you, Evan. How fucking dare you."

"I'm sorry, Travis. I've been trying to reach you the past couple of weeks, but you haven't been returning my calls," he says.

"The past couple weeks? You had hundreds of opportunities before that. You couldn't tell me then? Why did you tell me to hide who I am when you should have understood what I was going through? What I am still going through," I ask him while pointing my shaking finger in his face.

"Travis, look where you are right now. Do you think you would be here if they knew you were gay? Do you think you'd have this success outside the court? Do you think these multi-million-dollar companies would hire us to represent them? Why do you think there are no gay men at the top of their careers in professional sports? Hiding is the price we pay, and that is why I waited until now to come out, when the stakes are no longer high for me."

His explanation only serves to piss me off even more. I was young when I met him, and he had fed me this poison. Since he was one of the most accomplished players in our sport, I believed his advice was the only way to go about my career, so I listened to him.

"I don't care about the money. You could have made a difference to those young boys like me. You could have paved the way for us. But instead, you chose to hide behind your money," I say directly in his face.

"No one is that noble, Travis. Can you honestly say that you would rather be a trailblazer than a wealthy tennis legend? Give me a break," he says with a dry laugh.

That last comment makes me see red, and it takes all my self-control not to knock him on his ass.

"Watch me, Evan. Because unlike you, I will show all the young boys and girls out there that they can be who they want to be, regardless of who they love. And if that means losing it all, that is fucking okay with me."

I turn away from him to get out of his house, and I promise myself to never set foot in this fake fucker's place ever again. I pause for a second to give him one last piece of my mind.

"And Evan, I don't want to be a trailblazer or a tennis legend. I just want to be me. And it starts today."

"Travis, you're making a big mistake," he calls out.

"No, listening to you was my biggest mistake. This is the easiest decision I've ever made. Have a good life, Evan."

I couldn't wait to get away from him. I can't believe I listened to the venom that he's spewed all these years. I've overcome multiple break points in my career, but in my life, fear and cowardice have held me back. But not anymore. It's time to get back into the driver's seat of my life.

I feel like a brand-new person when I leave Evan's house, and I'm even more determined to prove him wrong. After hailing a taxi, I grab my phone out of my pocket and dial Aaliyah's number.

"Travis, where are you? I told you I was coming over," she scolds me the moment she answers my call.

"Long story, but I'm heading back. Stay there please. Also, how soon can you get a press conference organized?"

"Two hours. What's going on? I'm going to ask you one last time, is everything okay?"

"It is now. I'll tell you when I get there. Do you think Butch is available to give me a makeover? I look like shit."

"I'll give him a call. Get here and get here fast."

Chapter Twenty-Five

Aaliyah's head is leaning to one side and her arms are crossed over her chest while her foot taps repeatedly on the polished cement floor of my apartment when I walk in. She points to one of the bar stools by the counter and I follow her command while shaking my head. I pull the stool away from the kitchen island and sit down.

It's like a fog has been lifted and I can finally see clearly. This press conference needs to happen soon. I can't wait another minute to tell the world who I am and finally be with the man I love. I just hope it's not too late. I will do whatever it takes to live my life honestly, as well as try to get Ash back. I hope he will be proud of me. As much as I want to do this for me, this is also for him.

"What are you smiling about?" Aaliyah says, appraising me.

"I'm gay, and this press conference is to tell the world my truth." I say this with surprising ease considering this is the first time Aaliyah is hearing this admission. "I'm tired of hiding. I'm tired of lying to you and every other important person I care about. You may not want to represent me after this, but I hope we can stay friends. This is going to be a mess for you to clean up, but I can no longer pretend to be someone that I'm not."

She drums her fingers on the counter, lost in her

thoughts. I sit in suspense, waiting for what she has to say, hoping that she'll keep me as a client because I don't know if I can find someone as amazing as her. I also fear that she'll look at me differently.

A smile breaks out across her face and I release the breath that I had been holding.

"I'll never leave you as your agent, but more importantly, I will always be your friend. You know me better than that, Travis. I have been through everything with you—the ups, the downs, and all your achievements. I always felt like there was a piece of you that was missing. I am so happy to finally meet the whole you. I'm so proud of you and I'm glad you're going to free yourself from this burden. I knew you had been going through something. I can't even begin to tell you how touched I am that you chose to share this part of yourself with me."

I get up from the stool and Aaliyah meets me halfway, where we embrace. I cherish this moment with her. I can't believe how stupid I have been, listening to Evan St. John all these years rather than the people who care about me and love me. But as much as I want to blame Evan for everything, this is all on me. I can't change the past, but I can begin creating my future.

"What are we going to do now?" I ask Aaliyah with new-found determination.

"You're going to be fine. This is a different world,

Chapter Twenty-Five

Travis. Your fans are going to love you and you'll win even more people's hearts. Don't get me wrong, not everyone will support you, but you don't need them in your life. And I dare any company that you endorse to drop you. Imagine the shit they'll get! There is no good way to spin homophobia."

"You're right," I say. "When is the press conference? I need time to get ready."

"Look at you, you're gay for three minutes and you're acting like you cannot wait to be all dapper and everything. Butch will lose his shit when he finds out," she teases.

"You are something else. Want to help me find something to wear?" I ask.

"Whoa! You never ask for my help. I must say, I love the gay Travis way better than the uptight one."

"Hey! I take offense to that."

"Get used to it," she retorts.

We spend the next ten minutes looking for what Aaliyah calls the perfect coming-out outfit and decide on one of my designer navy-blue suits. I take a quick shower and put on sweatpants and my favorite UCLA t-shirt, since the plan is to have Butch work his magic on my hair and then change into the clothes we just picked.

"Ready?" Aaliyah asks when I walk out of my bedroom. "Our driver is waiting downstairs."

"I'm ready. Let's do this," I reply. "Aaliyah?"

She turns around. "Yeah?"

"Thank you for being cool about this. It means a lot to me."

"Of course, Boo," she says, blowing me an air kiss.

I fill Aaliyah in on my visit to Seattle, including about Ash, as we head downstairs. She asks a couple of questions about him and I also give her details about my coming-out chat with my parents. It feels really good to talk about it.

Chapter Twenty-Six
Ashton

I'm exhausted when I arrive in New York City and I'm still unsure if I'm doing the right thing.

Am I going to put my heart out there only to have it broken again? Maybe, but I need to know what has kept Travis in the closet all this time. I need him to tell me that it isn't because of me, and that it never has been about me. I need him to convince me that he doesn't feel the same way for me anymore. I need to hear it from him in order to move on, because I need to be able to tell myself that I tried everything.

I've only been to New York City twice in my life. The first trip was during a family vacation one spring when I was a teenager, and the other one was last year, when I watched Travis compete in the US Open final that he lost. I didn't tell anyone that I went, but after the match, I wished I hadn't. His anguish after losing in the final set in a tie-breaker made me want to run on the court and console him, and yank the trophy out of his opponent's hand. But I know that's not how it works.

The traffic is still how I remember it. I ask the taxi driver how much longer we have before we get to our destination, and he just waves me off and tells me that "we'll get there when we get there" in his very New York accent.

After booking the first flight out of Seattle to New York City, Katie drove me to Travis' parents' house to get his address. I didn't tell them why and their hopeful look convinced me an explanation was not necessary. I asked them not to tell Travis yet, because I wasn't sure if I could follow through with my plan.

"We're here," the driver says as he pulls over behind a black BMW. I give him thirty-five dollars for the fare and the tip, even though he doesn't deserve it.

I grab my duffel bag next to me and get out of the car, and the driver peels away the moment I close the door. I look up to verify the address on the building and before I even take my first step, a gentleman in a black uniform opens the door to the upscale building and Travis exits while talking to a gorgeous black woman.

My heart does a couple of somersaults and my anxiety level causes my stomach to drop. I think about

Chapter Twenty-Six

turning around and running away as fast as I can, but that is Travis' move, not mine, so I persevere.

"Trav!" I yell and he looks around. I don't doubt that he knows it's me because his eyes widen as he searches frantically. His eyes land on mine and, just like always, everything around us ceases to exist.

He rushes toward me, bumping pedestrians along the way, and when he reaches me, he encases me in his arms. "Ash, what are you doing here?" His voice is in my hair and his hold on me tightens.

"Travis, we have to go. We're going to be late," the woman says, probably thinking I'm some random fan on the street. She's even more stunning close up.

"Ash, this is my friend and agent, Aaliyah. Aaliyah, this is my Ash." I shake Aaliyah's hand and she gives me the sweetest smile. *My Ash.* Did Travis just say *my Ash*?

"Nice to meet you, Ash. Travis, why don't I take the front seat so you and your Ash can have the back seat." I don't miss the way she says *your Ash*.

I'm bewildered. Travis touches my back and guides me as we get inside the black BMW. My mind is all over the place, and when Travis kisses me the moment we're seated, I think for sure that I've gone crazy.

"I hope that kiss was okay?" he asks tenderly, seeing the shocked expression on my face.

"I like it. I actually love it, but what's going on? You're acting crazy?" I say, and I hear Aaliyah chuckle from the front seat. Travis pulls me in for another kiss, and I can feel him smile. He pulls away still holding both of my hands.

"Aaliyah set up a press conference for me, and I'm going to tell the world who I really am. No more hiding, no more lies."

"What? Why? Are you sure?" I ask.

"Yes. I'm tired of being a coward."

"Wait, you're going to a presser looking like this?" I ask, and a chorus of laughter echoes inside the cab.

"Of course not. Aaliyah has my suit."

"Oh! You know what? I think we should stop by the tuxedo rental place on the next block to get Ash's. You probably want to be photographed next to your man when he comes out, so you need to look like a million bucks," Aaliyah says, and before I can protest, we're parking and heading inside the store stocked with all types of suits and tuxedos.

My head is spinning from how fast everything is moving. Aaliyah is on a mission; she helps me pick out a suit while having multiple conversations on her cellphone about the press conference. I feel Travis squeeze my knee once we're back inside the car, making sure that I'm okay with all that's happening.

"Is this too much? I can have you dropped off at my

Chapter Twenty-Six

place if you like," Travis asks.

"It is too much," I say, and Travis' expression falls and his smile falters. "But I want to be with you when you do this. I want to be part of this."

"And I need you to be there too. Like I said earlier, no more hiding. Thank you, Ash."

"Oh my god, I'm going to be on the news!" I joke to assure Travis that I'm all in. I have waited for this for as long as I can remember, and I'm not about to miss this opportunity. I still can't believe this is happening. He's finally going to tell his truth.

"Yes, yes you are. Aren't you glad we got you a suit?" It's Aaliyah's turn to tease this time.

We pull over at the Sheraton Hotel and waste no time running toward the conference room. The room is filling with reporters and their camera crews, and when they get a glance of Travis, they start rushing in our direction.

"Go to the back door and I'll meet you there," Aaliyah instructs us as she interrupts their progress and redirects the group back to the ballroom.

A man wearing light makeup with his long hair pulled back into a bun greets us when we enter the back room that will serve as Travis' dressing room. There's a makeup table outlined with lights and the counter is covered with scissors, hair products, styling tools, and makeup.

"Butch, it's so nice to see you," Travis greets the man, and Butch giggles when Travis grabs his hand and kisses it gently. This should be humorous but for some reason, it makes me a little jealous. Something I've never felt before. I decide to grab Travis' hand, staking my ownership.

"And you, gorgeous man, must be the reason why Travis is having this press conference."

When Butch turns and walks toward his station to get ready, Travis is grinning so wide his face could split open. He turns and gives me a questioning look.

"What?" I ask innocently.

"Are you jealous?" he whispers.

"What? Don't be ridiculous."

"Yes, you are. It's okay. I think it's kind of hot," he says.

It doesn't take long for Butch to get Travis ready for his big announcement, and he gives me a quick makeover too, since I'll be sitting beside him.

A ringing sound coming from Travis' suit jacket grabs our attention and he answers it. "Okay, thanks," he says to who I assume is Aaliyah. He returns his look to me and says, "It's show time. The press is ready."

I sense his calm is a cover for what must be shattering nerves. "I'm proud of you, Travis. Regardless of the decisions you make today, I'm very proud of you," I say.

Chapter Twenty-Six

Travis takes a deep breath and I adjust his tie for the third time in the past three minutes. That earns me a wink and a kiss on my forehead.

"Let's do this, Dr. Kennedy."

Once we get to the conference room, Travis sits at the center of the table, while Aaliyah and I take the seats on each side of him. Travis doesn't beat around the bush and opens his statement with his admission that he is gay. Everyone gasps, and the flash of cameras and noise of reporters trying to speak over each other takes over the press conference. Aaliyah raises her hand to calm the pandemonium and uses her microphone to let everyone know that all their questions will be answered. She starts calling them one by one, and I can't believe how many ways and how many times you can ask someone how long they've been gay.

After everyone has the opportunity to ask Travis their questions, he prepares to give his final remarks, and the crowded room goes silent.

"I would like to thank you all for coming here today and allowing me to share my story with you. It took a while for me to get here, but I am so glad that I did. I was afraid for far too long, and I hurt many people along the way. It prevented me from having genuine relationships with those around me because I feared their judgment.

"I wish I could tell you that my experience is unique, but it isn't. There are thousands of people out there who are experiencing and feeling the same things as I did. Coming out is a very personal journey, and only you can decide when that moment is. No one should tell you when you're ready. You are the driver of your own life and when you decide it's time, be prepared to be disappointed, because not everyone around you will support your decisions or respect your choices. Surround yourself with those who will support you and give you the courage you need to keep going. Thank you all from the bottom of my heart."

Chapter Twenty-Seven
Travis

The ride back to my place after such a monumental afternoon was not what I had ever thought possible. I sure as hell had not envisioned Ashton sitting beside me holding my hand while New York City whizzed by. No one in the tennis world had started their day thinking, *What number-one player in the world might come out today?*

"Well, Dr. Kennedy, we're home." I squeeze Ash's hand when we pull up to my building.

"I'm actually nervous. I've seen your taste," he chuckles.

"You can rest your weary mind, baby, I'm loaded, so I hired a designer. You don't pay New York City prices and not have a baller flat!"

"Oh yeah, I forgot my boyfriend was the number-one tennis player on the planet. I guess I'll have to figure out what it's like dating royalty and all. I mean, you are the king of tennis, I've been told." Ash was in a light and fun mood.

"How about I give you a lifetime to figure it out? You can even take your time, if you'd like. I'm in no hurry now that I have you."

"Lead the way, your highness," Ashton states, motioning me to open the door.

I give my regular driver his usual huge tip.

"It makes me happy to see you happy, Mr. Montgomery," my driver says, moving his eyes to glance toward Ashton.

"Yes, my friend, I am very happy. Thank you."

I reach for Ash's hand and he hesitates for just a moment. "It's New York, Ash, and I plan to take advantage of my press conference. Now give me your hand."

I left in a rush earlier, so I hope my place looks presentable. I really want to impress Ashton on his first visit. I open the door and can see that, thankfully, the cleaner has been in and the place looks immaculate.

"You weren't kidding, Trav. Whoa. Who knew you had it in you?"

I beam from ear to ear as Ashton walks around, touching this and commenting on that. He's particularly impressed with my burgeoning art collection.

"Seriously, Trav, who's place is this?" He looks at me

Chapter Twenty-Seven

like I'm playing a prank on him. "It's gorgeous."

"Yeah? You like? Don't look too closely. It's all smoke and mirrors. Open a cabinet and you'll probably see paper plates and plastic wine glasses. I'm hardly ever here with the tour schedule I keep." I feel more self-conscious at his response to my place than I expected.

Ashton senses my slight embarrassment and walks across the room and grabs my hands. "It's terrific, Trav. It really is impressive."

We finish the tour and I walk into the kitchen to grab a bottle or two of something to use for a toast. I'll be sure to thank Aaliyah later for hiding two bottles of champagne in my fridge some time back. *You never know when you'll need this,* she'd said. She certainly was prescient that day.

I grab a bottle and, of course, I'd been right earlier, I only have plastic glasses.

"See? I told you, don't dig too deep." I hold up the bubbly and two cheap plastic wine glasses.

"What? You're not perfect? Call another presser, people. Mr. Numero Uno is normal!"

"You shit," I laugh and scoop Ash into my arms. "I love you."

Ashton tightens and becomes rigid in my arms. "Yeah, you heard me, Ashton Kennedy. I love you. And you know what else? I have always loved you. I could have told you that when we were sixteen."

"You do?" Ashton's eyes tear up, so I pull him tighter into my arms.

"Come with me, handsome. I'll show you just how much."

We walk hand-in-hand to my bedroom and place our wine glasses on a side table near the sitting area of the large room. "I'm going to take good care of you tonight. I've waited so many years to share a proper love-making session with the man of my dreams," I say in a low and steady cadence.

I assist Ash in removing his jacket. Another reason to thank Aaliyah later, as he looks so sexy in a suit. "Why have I never seen you in a suit? You're incredibly hot in one."

"Because we wasted six years," Ashton says, without anger.

"I'll make it up to you now, I promise," I growl into his ear.

I drop to my knees in front of Ash and unzip his pants. I don't bother with the belt or the button. I pull his thickening cock out of his boxers. As soon as my lips touch his cock, it throbs and swells. It's my turn to spoil my man.

I give him a slight nudge to sit back on the small sofa in my room and continue to swallow his cock. Once I have him splayed out on the sofa, I deep-throat him and really start to build up some momentum.

Chapter Twenty-Seven

I slide my mouth off him for a second to check on my progress.

"You like that, huh?" I mumble breathlessly.

I guess he does, because my only answer is a hand to the back of my head and a forceful push so he can shove his cock back into my throat. Ash is wiggling himself out of his suit pants, so I give him an assist and yank them and his boxers off. This gives me full access to his shaft, so I crawl right between his legs and continue to maneuver my mouth in that special way that I know drives him wild.

Ashton moans and expresses his desires by lifting his legs up and apart, giving me full access to his round, smooth, perfect ass.

"Not this way, baby. I want you on the bed, with me on top facing you, when I make love to you." I keep my voice low yet direct.

His eyes widen in an unexpected sort of way. You know, that look that says, *Oh yeah? I did not expect this, but oh yeah, I want whatever you're serving.*

I grab Ashton's hand and guide him to the bed. He sits on the edge in a fuzzy state of bliss while I undress slowly. His eyes admire me as I lose my clothes, one piece at a time for extra emphasis on what is about to come.

I step forward with a full erection and glance from his eyes to my cock. He gets the hint.

"Yeah, baby, that feels good. Suck your man. It's all yours." I aggressively grab the back of his head to maintain control of his mouth. "That's right, baby. Get me good and hard so I can show you how much I need to be inside you."

I stand still as Ashton reaches around and grabs my ass cheeks, pulling me deeper into his mouth and testing his gag reflexes. "Fuck, baby," I moan.

I know I need to be in him now or I'm going to shoot my first load too quick. I reach down and push his head off my cock, and he looks up at me with a questioning look on his face, as if to say, *We're not done here, are we?*

"I need to be inside you now," I growl.

Ash lays back on the bed and holds his hands above his head to let me know, without a doubt, that he wants me to take the lead. That's always been the thing with sex for us—we know each other and the roles that please us the most.

I crawl up his body, licking my way from his knees to a quick revisit of his cock, and then my mouth is pressed on his. I relax my weight on him and let our bodies find the grooves that fit. We're an amazing fit, and it shows again as I'm about to make love to the man I have chosen to admit my love to.

Ash pulls his knees up my sides and wraps his legs around my waist. "Someone's ready for his man," I say.

Chapter Twenty-Seven

"I'm always ready when it comes to taking care of your needs, stud," he moans.

I love this side of Ash. He's the brains in this operation and can come across as a bit quiet and scholarly. But when it comes to sex, he's a completely different man.

"Come on, Trav, put it in me."

I grab the lube from my nightstand and lather a generous amount on my cock, then press it against his entrance. He's as welcoming as I'd figured he'd be, and as horny as I am. I feel my erection slide into his tight, sweet ass.

"That's it, baby, damn you're tight." I moan softly as I hold his legs up and watch my cock disappear into his waiting hole. He rocks back and forth as I move in, gently at first, knowing that soon I'll be plowing him hard, just the way he craves.

Our eyes lock as I'm moving in and out of him. Our bodies are joined as one and it has never felt more right than it does now. I slowly move my cock in and out of his smooth ass, and watch the pleasure in his eyes as he takes all of me. His moaning gets louder as my pace quickens. Ash pulls my ass toward him, demanding that I don't stop the building rhythm.

"You feel so amazing inside me, Travis," he moans.

I rest his legs over my shoulders, grab his cock in my lubed hand and stroke it. My cock is driving in deeper as I stroke his dick in time with my plunges.

"Keep this up and I'm going to shoot, stud," he says, gritting his teeth as I continue to violate his asshole.

I slam into him over and over again, and feel his cock expanding as he is about to come. "Oh yeah, that's it," he moans.

His head is tossing back and forth in ecstasy as my own orgasm is building.

"Are you ready? I'm going to shoot my load in your hot ass," I growl, as I drive my cock in as deep as I can, my balls slapping against his exposed ass. "Fuck!" I moan. My load is pulsing up my shaft as I feel Ash tense and tighten his legs. "It's coming baby. It's fucking coming!" I fill his ass with my load and grip his cock tighter as I witness his own orgasm spray out of him and all over his chest. I collapse onto him, sweating and still catching my breath after our aggressive love-making. There is no doubt how I feel about Ashton Kennedy. "I love you, Ash," I whisper.

Ash leans forward and wraps his arms around my neck, pulling himself as close as he can. Our lips come together, and he returns my words directly into my mouth. "I love you, Travis Montgomery."

The next day I think back to all that transpired the previous day. The press conference was beyond what I thought I would ever be able to do, and having Ashton by my side while the entire sports world looked on was even better.

Chapter Twenty-Seven

The text messages had started coming in immediately. My parents were the first to text and their message was short and sweet: *Call us!* They were also the second text: *We love you and are so proud of you.* I finally told Aaliyah to handle all my well wishes and to not bother responding to the hate messages. As it turned out, there were virtually none of those. Evan even sent a message through his publicist that simply said: *I'm rooting for you.* Whatever that means.

I don't need Evan's support, and even though I hate to admit it, looking back, I can thank him for giving me the kick in the ass to wake up and take control of my own life. I have Ashton with me now. I can and will overcome all challenges with his strength cheering me on.

But most of all, I'm finally free.

Epilogue
Travis

Australian Open 2020. Men's Final. Fifth set, 5-4, 40-love, championship point.

This is it. My dream of winning all the major tennis tournaments, a career Grand Slam, depends on this moment. *You've got this*, I murmur to myself as I wait for the nerves to overwhelm my emotions, just like before. But it doesn't come this time. Instead, a profound feeling of contentment takes residence in my already full heart and I welcome it.

The reason why is sitting a few feet from where I'm standing. Ash. Who currently looks like a nervous wreck. His shaking hands rest on his legs, which are bouncing up and down, the perfect representation of his emotions these past four hours. I can't help but smile, and before positioning to serve, I give him a wink to assure him that everything will be all right.

Epilogue

It's amazing how quickly life changes. If you had told me four months ago when I'd won the US Open that I would be serving for another major championship win with the love of my life in the player's box, cheering for me, I would have told you that you'd gone mad. But that is exactly where I am now. It wasn't easy, but I'm here.

The noise of the crowd takes me out of my musing. Just like always, they are yelling my name repeatedly as excitement fills the air. Everyone is on their feet and dozens of media outlet cameras are aimed in my direction.

You've got this, I tell myself one more time, before touching the silver tennis racket pin on my shirt collar.

I position to hit my serve. I bounce the ball eight times out of habit, toss it in the air, then strike a 135-mph serve.

"Fault!" the line judge yells.

I glance at Ash, and if I were not about to serve for another championship, I would have laughed at the way he is biting every fingernail he has.

I follow the same routine but this time, I hit my serve with a slower pace and with more spin. But instead of landing on the other side of the net, it lands in the net.

"Fault!"

I have just served a double fault, giving my opponent the point.

"Forty-15," the umpire says into his microphone.

I walk to the ad side of the court to serve once again. With the same routine, I hit another serve.

"Fault!"

"Not again," I mumble.

"Second serve," the chair umpire says.

The collective sigh and heavy whispering reverberate around the stands. I glance at Ash once again to remind myself that, win or lose, I will always have him. He holds his fist up in the air urging, me to finish this match. I see him smile, and that's all I need to relax.

I position myself once again and prepare for my second serve, which normally would be slower than my first. But I have another idea. I touch the silver tennis racket on my shirt, bounce the ball eight times, and hit the fastest serve I can, not caring if it gives me another double fault.

The radar reads the serve as 225 kph, which is approximately 140 mph. The crowd gasps and my opponent hits the blistering serve back to my side of the court, where it sails past the baseline where I'm standing.

"Out!" the line judge yells.

"Game, set, match, Travis Montgomery," the chair umpire says.

I throw my racket in the air and lay back onto the court as the Melbourne crowd erupts. After a few

Epilogue

celebratory moments, I walk to the net to thank my opponent. He's a good friend, so we hug it out and he congratulates me.

After grabbing something from my bag, I make my way to my player's box. Everyone tries to give me high fives and fist bumps, or attempts to shake my hand, but my sight is focused on Ash. He's giving me a look that says, *What are you doing?*

It takes a few minutes to get to him, but when I do, I kiss him with all my might, not caring that the world can see. Because for the first time in my life, I am not afraid. I wipe the tears that are flowing down his cheeks with my thumbs, and that seems to make him cry even more. And because I am me and I can't leave well enough alone, I drop to one knee.

A collective gasp echoes around the stadium. Ash's eyes widen and his mouth follows suit.

I have been waiting for the perfect moment to propose to him, and after so many years, this seems like the perfect occasion.

"Will you marry me?" I ask. He nods—*yes*—and the crowd erupts like I have never seen or heard before.

It took a while for me to realize that the greatest win of my life was the moment eight years ago when I kissed Ash for the first time, but I was stupid enough to let him go. I won't make that mistake again. From this moment on, the winning will be so much sweeter.

The End

Acknowledgment

I could not have done this without all of you. This over used cliché has never been more true than this past year. To my family and friends who have been my greatest cheerleaders from the very beginning of this new adventure, Thank you!

To my mom and dad who think that my book will be more successful than the Harry Potter Series (bless their hearts). To my sisters and brothers, I love all of you and please skip the following pages... I don't think you will be able to handle the heat. LOL

To every independent author out there- the kindness and support you've shown this writer is more than I could have ever asked for.

To all the bloggers, influencers and book fanatics who helped me spread the word about Break Point, Thank you. Travis and Ashton's story was able to touch people's lives because of your tenacity. This is for you.

Jennifer Griffin and Carlie Slattery, my amazing editor and proofreader, thank you for helping me complete a story that I can be proud of. Sophie Hanks, thank you for always accommodating my needs.

To my dear friend Katie, thank you for allowing me to use our real-life friendship as an inspiration to Ashton and Katie's bond.

To Sam, Dar, Carol, Denice, Elle, Reenie and Sue. I must have done something great in my past life to be able to have your unyielding love and support. Thank you again for the campfire listening sessions!

Made in the USA
Monee, IL
13 August 2021